Christopher Reynolds has been the reigning British cage fighter champion for the past two consecutive years. The next time he goes into the cage to defend his title, he demonstrates to his opponent in the first few minutes why he's earned the nickname, Raging Reynolds. Christopher is fired up and on good form. His opponent's blood is shed, and it's more than his male ego and pride on the line. When it looks like Christopher's about to seal his victory, he freezes, puts his hand to his throat and collapses on the floor. When he's pronounced dead and high levels of heroin are found in his bloodstream, foul play is suspected. Unable to go to the police, Christopher's bereaved long-term partner, Ethan, turns to the Apparition Intervention team for help. As the ex-female karate champion in her county, Jane is the obvious person to investigate the case. The spirit of a junkie comes to her aid and leads her to a potential culprit, but when she gets too close to them, she finds herself in the cage with them, and then she's the one fighting for her life so that justice can be served.

Cage Fighter
Copyright © 2019 LJ Collins
ISBN: 978-1-4874-2429-9
Cover art by Martine Jardin

Published by eXtasy Books Inc or
Devine Destinies, an imprint of eXtasy Books Inc

Look for us online at:
www.eXtasybooks.com or www.devinedestinies.com

Cage Fighter
Apparition Intervention
Book 3

By

LJ Collins

DEDICATION

This book is dedicated to Polly Duffee – even though after thirty-five years of friendship I still prefer to call her Paula and she loathes me for it lol. Where do I start? We've drifted in and out of each other's lives, but we've always known that we've been there for each other and on call in times of need. We've spent some of the most amazing times and years together on this journey called life – and my life wouldn't be complete without you. I admire you for your strength as a woman who has fought against the odds to get where you are now. I'm so proud of you and what you've achieved. For that reason it seemed very fitting to dedicate this book, Cage Fighter, to you – you've never been in a cage, but you're definitely a fighter. I'll never forget our time in Chelsea, London, and I will write The Thursday Club one day – a story about our lives that will never be forgotten and cherished forever. Love you and the rest of the Thursday Club members dearly. All of you mean the world to me. LYL. LJ. Xxx

CHAPTER ONE

It was fight night again, and as Ethan gripped the steering wheel, it became increasingly clammy. He did his best to focus on the road ahead and control the car as well as he could so he wouldn't kill himself and Christopher before they'd arrived at their destination, but his heart beat faster as he drove along the approach road to where the fight was going to take place. The nearer they got, the more erratic and uncontrollable his breathing became. He breathed in deeply through his nose, then exhaled slowly through his mouth.

The giant yellow dwarf star that bathed Earth with light, energy and heat on a daily basis glowed brightly in the distance. It looked enchanting surrounded by an orange aura that was eventually consumed by the onset of the evening darkness. It gracefully disappeared on the horizon when Ethan and Christopher arrived at the sooty grey disused brick warehouse where Christopher was going to be fighting for his life again. Ethan swallowed hard and wanted to stop the car so he could find a paper bag and place it over his mouth and nose.

Christopher put a reassuring hand on Ethan's forearm. "Look. I can sense that you're nervous, but relax. Everything's going to be fine."

As much as Ethan wanted to, it was beyond him. When the two attendants had opened the gates to the warehouse car park, he looked in front of him, and the only form of life he could see were ugly bunches of green weeds that had sprung up in between the cracks in the surface of the grey concrete.

1

Ethan passed through the gates and drove to the back of the warehouse. He parked as quickly as he could by the entrance door. He looked at it and turned to Christopher. "Gees. I've got butterflies in my stomach, and I feel as sick as a dog." He opened the car door, leaned to his right, and started retching. Thankfully nothing came out, but it left his stomach muscles tight and strained.

Ethan always got nervous before a fight even though he knew Christopher hadn't been beaten in any of his fights during the past two years. Ethan snuggled into Christopher, who put a reassuring arm around his shoulder.

Christopher pecked him on the lips. "Don't get so uptight. I know who I'm up against and I'm confident I'll be able to knock him out in the first few minutes."

As much as Ethan wanted to believe him, and had every confidence in Christopher, there was a nagging doubt and concern in the back of Ethan's mind that he might lose more than just the fight.

Christopher was competing in another illegal cage fight, and unlike the televised professional fights, the illegal fights were a lot more brutal, and they were no-holds-barred. Some of the men never made it out of the cage alive, and that was Ethan's biggest fear — that he'd lose the love of his life before the night was over.

Ethan looked around the car park. "Judging by the number of cars here, it looks like the fight has attracted a big crowd. There's always a big crowd when you're fighting and given you're defending your title that has remained intact for the past two years, I guess the crowds have flocked in to find out if you're going to be defeated."

Christopher chuckled. "Well, you know as well as I do, the spectators are divided when it comes to me. There are those who love the fact that I, as an openly gay man, knock the shit out of straight macho guys, and there are those who despise me for it. Especially my opponents because it dents their male egos to be annihilated by a gay man—or a queer or poof as I'm often referred to behind my back."

Ethan snorted. "Yeah, but no man in their right mind would have the courage to call you that to your face because they'd be instantly knocked out. It's always puzzled and intrigued me why heterosexual men invariably stereotype gay men as being camp and weak. I'm really proud of you for completely shattering that image of gay men by consistently demonstrating that a gay man can fight just as well—if not better—than any heterosexual man no matter how butch and burly they are."

Christopher leaned into Ethan and pecked him on his cheek. "Why, thank you. That means a lot coming from you. Anyway, let's get in there, so I can get this fight over and done with."

As they walked toward the entrance, two security guards were standing by the door. They beckoned Ethan and Christopher to follow them and led them down a dimly lit and dingy corridor.

Ethan shuddered, and the hairs on his forearms stood on end when he heard the distant sound of the master of ceremonies talking to the crowd and getting them fired up before the fight. "And challenging the reigning champion tonight is *Desmond the Destroyer*." The crowd cheered and shouted out their words of support and encouragement. And of course, the reigning champion is Christopher. Otherwise known as *Raging Reynolds*." There was a roar of cheering, which was quickly met with booing.

A man in the crowd shouted out, "Desmond's gonna destroy that poof tonight."

The roars of laughter that ensued echoed around the warehouse and other members of the audience started chanting, "Desmond's gonna destroy that poof tonight!"

Christopher looked at Ethan and chuckled. "Looks like I'll have to knock the shit out of Desmond the Destroyer as quickly as I can to shut those bigoted fuckers up."

Ethan laughed nervously and reached for Christopher's hand. "You do that so we can get out of here as soon as possible and go and have a nice relaxing meal."

Christopher stopped, turned toward Ethan, placed his hands on the back of his head, and pecked him on his forehead. "Yeah. That sounds like a plan. I fancy a nice Chinese. What about you?"

Ethan looked up at Christopher and smiled. "That suits me fine. Just make sure you get the better of him before he has the chance to get the better of you. And I hope that once you've won this fight, you'll give up the cage fighting. You've more than proved your point, so walk away from it while you still can."

Christopher pecked Ethan on his lips and smiled. "I promise. Just this one last fight, and then I'll call it a day and get a sensible job as a bodyguard or bouncer."

They reached a doorway, and one of the bouncers pointed toward it. "This is where you'll be getting changed. The fight starts in ten minutes. We'll be waiting outside so when you're ready we'll escort you to the cage. Oh, and good luck. I think you might need it tonight. Desmond the Destroyer is after your blood, and he's vowed not to leave the cage until he's shed it."

Christopher snorted and shrugged his shoulders. "Yeah, whatever. If I had a pound for every time I've heard that I'd be a very rich man."

The bouncer winked at Christopher and chuckled. "I'm sure you would be, man, and I admire you for taking him on. He's got a huge chip on his shoulder, so I hope you can knock it off and teach him a lesson."

Christopher patted the bouncer on his shoulder and

winked. "You know what they say . . . the bigger they are the harder they fall and all that shite."

"You got it, man."

Ethan and Christopher walked into the room that still had a desk, chair, and other office equipment in it that was covered in dust and cobwebs.

Christopher took his trainers, jeans and t-shirt off and put them in the locker on his right. He looked as powerful and fierce as a British bulldog as he stood in the middle of the room in just his underwear.

Ethan reached into Christopher's gym bag and grabbed his white shorts and fighting gloves. He handed them to Christopher, and he put them on.

As Ethan walked toward the door, he felt Christopher's hands on his shoulders. He turned around to face him. "Look. I know I say this to you every time before I go into the cage, but just in case I don't come out of it, I want you to know that I love you with all my heart. If it wasn't for you, I wouldn't have the strength, drive and determination to do this. I do it for you so we can have a better and more comfortable life together."

Ethan looked up at Christopher and winced. "Please don't say that. I know you do, but it makes me feel guilty every time you say it. Come on — get out there and kick that guy's arse so we can get out of here and have a nice romantic meal together."

Christopher embraced Ethan and kissed him on his forehead. "You got it. Right. Let's do this and make our bank balance a lot healthier so we can take a nice holiday somewhere."

Ethan fixed his gaze on Christopher's. "That would be nice. And it goes without saying that you know that I love you, and maybe we could make that holiday our honeymoon?"

Christopher teasingly slapped Ethan on his backside. "Now that gives me all the more reason to want to take this dude out as quickly as I can. Would you really commit to having a civil partnership with me?"

"Of course I would, so make sure you get out of that cage alive and tomorrow we can start looking at rings and making the arrangements."

Christopher took hold of Ethan's hands and bent down on one knee. "Ethan Cartwright, will you make me a proud man and marry me?"

The tears in Ethan's eyes welled up. He looked down at Christopher, smiled, and nodded. "I will. You're my man and my world, and I don't even want to imagine what my life would be like without you in it. I will, I will, I will."

Christopher stood up and embraced Ethan. "Well, that's settled then. We'll start making the arrangements tomorrow. Now I have to go and kick some arse, and I've never been so motivated to do it."

There was a knock on the door, and the door latch clicked. Ethan turned around, and Christopher's trainer, Dan, was standing in the doorway. "Hi, guys. I hope I'm not interrupting anything but the fight starts in five minutes, and I wanted to have a quick chat with Christopher before he goes into the cage."

"Fire away," Christopher said. "You know you can say anything in front of Ethan."

"Yeah, sure. I just wanted to make sure you were geared up for the fight. Desmond the Destroyer is looking in good shape, but don't let his height and size advantage intimidate you. He may be bigger than you, but you're more agile and faster than he is, so use those strengths to your advantage."

"You got it, Dan. I can't wait to get in the cage and show him why people call me *Raging Reynolds*. I'll get in quick, so he doesn't have time to think and use that strength of his against me."

"That's my boy. I have every confidence you'll run rings

around him, and he'll go down like a sack of potatoes."

Christopher laughed and punched the air with his right hand. "That's the plan, Dan."

"Right then. Are you ready to go?"

"Yep. I'm as ready as I'll ever be. Me and Ethan have just decided to get married, so I'm feeling a bit soppy at the moment. I need to get in the cage and stare Desmond the Destroyer in the eyes to get myself fired up."

Dan looked down at the floor and opened his mouth to speak, but nothing came out. After a momentary pause, he looked up at Ethan and Christopher, held his hands out to his side and smiled. "Well, that's great news. But as you said, you need to get yourself fired up and focus on taking Desmond the Destroyer out. If you can do that, we'll all be onto a nice little earner this evening. There's a lot of money riding on you, and if you win, you'll get your usual cut."

"Yep. Well if Ethan and I are going to get married, we're sure gonna need that money."

"Right then. Let's get going, and I'll give you a little pep talk as we make our way to the cage so you can get into the fighting spirit."

Christopher tugged on his gloves and smacked his hands together in front of him. Ethan had never really understood why the fighters bothered wearing the gloves because apart from a slight bit of padding on the knuckles, they were pretty standard gloves that people used at the gym. Christopher had told him they helped soften the blow on his knuckles and his opponent, but he couldn't see how.

They left the room and turned right into the dimly lit corridor. As they approached the main warehouse, the cheers and boos of the crowd got louder and more intimidating. Ethan did his best to convince himself Christopher would be fine, and the noise added to the atmosphere and tension for the crowd and the fighters. Without it, the fighters wouldn't get as fired up as they needed to be to step into the cage.

Christopher and Dan walked in front of Ethan. Dan had an arm around Christopher's shoulder, and Ethan could see he was leaning into Christopher and talking to him. Christopher shook his head and started punching the air with both hands, so Ethan assumed that Dan was giving him his pep talk to get him fired up and aggressive.

When Christopher and Dan walked into the warehouse, the master of ceremonies must have seen them enter. "And joining us now is the reigning champion, Raging Reynolds, who's come to defend his title." A mixture of cheering and booing echoed around the warehouse and bounced off the walls and windows, creating an almost deafening atmosphere of hysteria.

Ethan took his mobile phone out of his trouser pocket and scrolled through the icons until he found the video button. He hit it and held his mobile phone out in front of him so he could record the moment Christopher entered the cage and the fight.

Ethan always recorded Christopher's fights because it gave him something else to focus on, so he wasn't constantly worrying about one of Christopher's opponents getting the better of him. Christopher also liked to watch the video recordings time and time again so he could study his opponents, their moves, his moves and both the fighter's reactions.

Desmond the Destroyer was already in the cage. Judging by the way he paced around shaking his head and arms, Ethan suspected he was a little apprehensive but anxious for the fight to start so both he and Christopher would know which way it was going to go.

Ethan imagined that Desmond the Destroyer was as nervous as any of Christopher's previous opponents had been before a fight. They all knew what damage Christopher was capable of, even to guys who were much bigger than him.

They feared not only the pain they'd have to endure, but the shame they'd have to confront after the fight if a gay man knocked the shit out of them and won it. If they made it out of the cage alive, they'd be ridiculed and mocked not only by the crowd but by their trainer, family, and friends.

Christopher and Dan stopped when they reached the cage door. Dan handed him a frosted blue sports bottle which Ethan assumed contained water or a high energy drink. Christopher took a slug of whatever was in the bottle, screwed his face up and handed it back to Dan.

Dan put an arm around Christopher's shoulder, leaned into him and whispered what Ethan assumed were some final words of encouragement to boost his ego and get him even more fired up.

Christopher stepped into the cage and Ethan followed Dan to the outside perimeter and stood beside him. He zoomed the camera out a bit so he could see both of the fighters who were standing in bare feet, shorts and their gloves.

He tilted the camera down so he could see the bloodstains on the floor that had been left from the previous two fights, and it was a grim reminder that the cage fighters didn't mess around — they went for the kill and only the last man standing walked out of the cage. The other one was taken out on a stretcher.

Christopher and Desmond fixed their gazes on each other, and they both looked as determined as the other to take their opponent out.

Desmond the Destroyer was about four inches taller than Christopher, and his huge muscular frame was intimidating. Christopher had never fought him before so Ethan was concerned that if Christopher took a direct punch or kick, it would be enough to take him out.

As Ethan focused on the screen, it was shaking slightly, so he supported his right arm with his left hand. His heart pounded, and he wasn't sure if he wanted to go into the cage and drag Christopher out of it or for the fight to begin as soon as possible so he'd know if Christopher was skilful and fast enough to dominate and destroy the destroyer.

The referee, Mike, who was better known as *Mike, the medicine man*, on the cage fighting scene, stepped in between the two fighters and pushed his arms out to his side. Despite Mike being much shorter and round than the fighters, both of them stepped back, and Mike stepped back to the edge of the cage. A buzzer sounded loudly, and it signified the fight could start.

Christopher and Desmond stepped forward, held out their right hands and tapped their knuckles together. They both stepped back and eyed each other up, no doubt waiting to see who was going to make the first move and attack.

After a couple of seconds, Christopher looked at Ethan, twitched his head and winked. He turned to face Desmond the Destroyer and surged forward with his left hand held out in front of him for defence and his right hand back, so it was ready to strike. He pounced toward Desmond the Destroyer who put his hands in front of his face to block any punches.

Desmond raised a leg to kick Christopher, but he was too quick, and he broke through Desmond's defence and showered him with left and right hooks to the side of his head and stomach. When Desmond leaned forward slightly to protect himself, Christopher grabbed him around the back of his head, raised his right knee sharply and kneed him under his chin. Desmond's head flew back, and Christopher kneed him in the stomach and punched him repeatedly in the face.

Desmond reached his arms out, grabbed Christopher around the waist and pulled him close to him. He wrapped his arms around Christopher's lower back and squeezed him hard. Christopher's range and movements were restricted, and while he tried to knee Desmond in the leg and beat him on the side of his head, Desmond head-butted him.

Christopher blew out air and shook his head rapidly. Then he retaliated by head-butting Desmond on his nose. Within seconds the blood flowed out of it, and he loosened his grip on Christopher a bit, giving him slightly more range and movement.

As Desmond shook his head, his blood sprayed all over Christopher's face and body, but he was relentless. Christopher raised his knee and kneed Desmond in the crotch. Desmond released his grip on Christopher all together, leaned forward and grabbed his injured privates.

Christopher took a step back, turned to his side and leaned back on his left leg. He raised his right knee and kicked out hard. His foot hit Desmond on the side of his head, and he was knocked off his feet. There was a loud thud, and the sprung floor of the cage vibrated when his immense body crashed against it.

Christopher seized his opportunity to go for the knockout. With the speed of a cheater, he leapt toward Desmond, crouched down on one knee and pounded his face and head with his fists.

Mike ran toward Christopher and pulled him away from Desmond, who was out cold. That signified Christopher had won the fight and that Mike had wanted to stop Christopher beating Desmond until he was dead.

Christopher tapped the referee's hands that were on his chest, and the referee released his grip. Christopher turned to Ethan and Dan, raised his hands in the air and started running toward them. Ethan was elated he looked so happy and that he was clearly buzzing and on a high from his victory.

When he was a few steps away, Christopher stopped, crouched forward and put his left hand to his throat and placed his right hand over his heart. Foam spewed out of his mouth, and he coughed violently. Ethan instinctively knew that something terrible was happening.

He turned to Dan. "We have to do something. He's not right."

Dan grabbed hold of Ethan's arm. "I'm sure he's fine. Give him a few minutes to recover. He probably got a bit too over excited and needs to calm down a bit."

"For Christ sake, Dan. He's foaming at the fucking mouth. Would you call that normal?"

"Ethan. Just calm down and give him a few minutes. I'm sure he'll be fine. That was a hard blow to his head, and he needs time to recover."

Ethan turned to look at Christopher. He raised his head slightly, and his wide eyes, frothing mouth and contorted face indicated he was in a state of panic. He reached out his right hand and tried to take a step forward, but his knees buckled, and he fell forward. The thud of his body and head hitting the sprung floor broke the hushed silence in the warehouse.

CHAPTER TWO

Ethan looked on in horror as Mike ran toward Christopher and turned him onto his side. Vomit spewed out of his mouth, and his body appeared to be lifeless. Ethan ran toward the entrance of the cage and tried to pull the door open, but it had been locked from the inside—a normal practice to stop anybody getting into the cage while the fight was taking place. He pulled and pushed against the door willing it to open, but it refused to cooperate.

Ethan turned to Dan and frantically looked around at the crowd who were rapidly dispersing and heading toward the exit. "Call an ambulance. Somebody—anybody—call an ambulance!" He looked into the cage and Mike had rolled Christopher onto his back and was pressing his cupped hands on his chest rapidly. "Try giving him mouth to mouth resuscitation." Mike looked up at Ethan and shrugged his shoulders. "Well, if you won't do it open the door, and I'll do it."

Mike frantically pressed his cupped hands against Christopher's chest, and after a few seconds, he looked at Ethan and held his hands out to his sides. He stood up, walked toward the door and opened it. "I'm afraid he's gone. I tried to do what I could, but I don't even think an ambulance team would have made it here in time to save him. I'm really sorry."

Ethan ran toward Christopher and threw himself down on his knees at his side. He cupped his hands and pressed them against his chest. He covered Christopher's parted lips with his, breathed in through his nose and blew air into his mouth. He did it several times, and despite the dreadful taste and slimy feel of Christopher's vomit against his lips, he was determined not to give up.

Several minutes passed, and Christopher showed no signs of responding to his CPR treatment or mouth to mouth resuscitation. Ethan cupped his head in his hands and leaned forward to kiss him on the mouth. Tears streamed from his eyes and burned them.

Ethan swallowed hard and gasped for breath, knowing he had to accept Christopher was dead, and there was nothing that he, or anybody else, could do to bring him back to life.

Ethan looked down at Christopher and shook his head. There were so many questions running through his mind and so much agony in his heart and mind they both ached — an intense pain he'd never experienced before and a pain he didn't know if he'd ever recover from.

Somebody's hands rubbed Ethan's shoulders. He turned around and looked up. Dan was stood behind him. "And where the fuck have you been?" Ethan screamed. "Why didn't you do anything? We might have been able to save him if we'd done something. But no — you told me he'd be fine, and now he's fucking dead."

"Ethan. This is hitting me as hard as it is you. Christopher was like a son to me, so I'm just as devastated as you are. We're all in shock because this has come as a complete surprise, but without wishing to sound too harsh, we need to get Christopher's body out of here before the police arrive. They're bound to turn up at some point, and if they find us and him here then we're all going to be under fire and have a whole lot of difficult questions to answer, and it's quite probable we'll all end up spending the rest of our days behind bars."

Ethan wanted to scream at Dan and punch and kick him, but he knew he was right. They had to get Christopher and themselves out of the warehouse before the police arrived. It only took one member of the crowd to call them, and they'd have been there in a shot. He mustered up all the strength he could and looked at Dan. "Yeah. I know you're right. But we need to make arrangements for an autopsy to be completed so we can find out what happened to Christopher. I don't know . . . he just had this strange look in his eyes when he last looked at me, so I need to know what his cause of death was."

Dan held out a hand and took Ethan's. "Come here. I've already made the one and only phone call I need to make. A friend of mine who's an undertaker is on his way to collect the body, and he'll make arrangements for an autopsy to be completed. We all know him, and we all use him in situations like this. He can be trusted to deal with it as discretely as humanly possible. It'll cost, but I'll take care of it, and I'll make sure you get what's left over from Christopher's share of the prize money."

"Thanks, Dan. I appreciate that and what you're doing. I don't know whether I'm coming or going at the moment, so it's reassuring to know you're taking care of things."

"Hey. We're family, right? So think nothing of it. Are you in a fit state to drive, or do you want me to get somebody to drive you home?"

"I'll be fine. I'll wait until the undertaker has picked up Christopher's body and then I'll go back to our place. Well . . . what used to be our place – it's gonna be a very strange night being there on my own, but it'll be the best place for me. Can you let me have the details of the undertaker and where Christopher's body is being taken to? I'd like to see him in the chapel of rest before the funeral."

"Of course. Consider it done. I'll send you a text with his name, number and address when I get home. I've got his phone number in my phone, but that's all."

"That's fine. So long as I have it tomorrow, that'd be great."

They had to wait about twenty minutes before the under-taker, and his team arrived with a stretcher. Dan greeted them and beckoned them with his hand. The men lifted Christopher onto the stretcher, picked it up and made their way out of the cage. Ethan wanted to run after them because he couldn't bear to be parted from Christopher. But he knew in the back of his mind it would have been pointless. Christopher was dead, and he had to get used to life without him.

Once the undertaker and his team had left the warehouse, Ethan said goodbye to Dan and made his way toward the exit. His mind and body were numb as he walked past the room where Christopher had got changed. He would have paid any price to have been able to turn back the hands of time to that moment. To be given the opportunity to talk Christopher out of going into the cage, and convincing him they should have left, gone for a nice romantic meal and started planning their wedding the following day. But he'd missed his opportunity, and it would never be presented to him again.

Ethan got into the car and turned the ignition on. The sound of Caron Wheeler singing *I Adore You* filled his ears and the reality of what had happened hit him with the force of a sledgehammer. Less than an hour ago, he and Christopher had been listening to the song while Ethan had driven them to the warehouse. Ethan sobbed and covered his face with his hands.

It was one of their favourite songs because it reflected the way they'd felt for each other, and Ethan was consumed by a sickening sense of loss, loneliness, bitterness about what had happened and anger toward himself for allowing Christopher to go into the cage.

It may have been the song, or it could have been that Ethan was sat in the car on his own, but he was hit with a wave of sadness, and there was nothing he could do to stop the tears streaming from his eyes. He couldn't bear the thought of

going back to what had been his and Christopher's home —
seeing all the photos of them together, being reminded of all
the wonderful years they'd spent together, having to spend
the evening there alone, and go to bed on his own.

The thought that scared Ethan most was that he wouldn't
be able to face his future without Christopher, and he'd be
tempted to take an overdose of sleeping tablets so he
wouldn't have to wake up the following morning and confront the pain and misery he suspected awaited him. He
wanted to be at rest with Christopher, so neither one of them
would have to confront a life of loneliness and grieving.

Ethan knew in the back of his mind that taking his own life
would be the last thing Christopher would have wanted him
to do. Even though it struck him as being the easiest option,
he had to find an inner strength from somewhere and deal
with his loss.

He was pretty sure their families and friends would give
him all the emotional and moral support he'd need, but dealing with the ongoing long-term emotions and mental scars
would be down to him to deal with.

Ethan wiped the tears away from his eyes, put the car into
gear and started to drive toward the exit. As much as he was
dreading going back home, he didn't want to be near the place
where Christopher had lost his life.

When the song *I Adore You* finished *Don't Quit* by Caron
Wheeler started playing and Ethan took that as a sign from
Christopher in Heaven that he had to be strong and cope with
the aftermath of what had happened.

As Ethan drove along the only exit road from the warehouse, he was relieved that no police cars passed him and
longed to get home, have a stiff drink, and try to think about
what had happened a bit more rationally so he could try and
come to terms with it.

While Ethan was driving along the motorway, the vision of

Christopher foaming at the mouth kept flashing through his mind. He tried to block it out, but it kept coming back to haunt him. As disturbing as it was, Ethan started to wonder what had caused such a strange thing to happen. He'd never seen anybody foaming at the mouth before so he was curious to understand what had provoked it. He did his best to reassure himself that the autopsy report would give him the answer to his question.

When Ethan got home, he went to the drinks cabinet and grabbed a bottle of scotch. He went to the kitchen, poured a generous measure into a glass and took a large slug. The alcohol burned his throat, but it filled him with a warming sensation, and he knew it would help him relax a bit within a matter of minutes.

Ethan went to the lounge and sat down on one of the armchairs. He looked around the room, and it painfully lacked the sight, sound, and cheer of Christopher. Ethan knew if he pondered on Christopher's absence too long, he'd unconsciously slip into a deep black hole that he might never be able to climb out of.

Ethan shook his head which snapped him out of the powerful hypnotic trance he was dangerously giving into. To distract himself, he reached for his laptop on the coffee table and booted it up. He wanted to listen to some music to try and help him relax, so he could steer his mind away from the dark and disturbing thoughts rushing through it before they took permanent control and pushed him over the edge—to the point of no return—insanity.

He knew he had to call Christopher's mother, Sylvia, to break the horrifying news to her, but it was gone eleven at night, and he knew she'd most likely have been in bed. He didn't want to disturb her and cause her a traumatic night, but he knew she would never forgive him if he didn't let her know.

Ethan put his laptop back on the coffee table and reached for his mobile phone. He scrolled through his contact list until he found Sylvia's home phone number. He pressed the call button and gritted his teeth.

The phone rang and rang, but there was no answer, and the answerphone prompted him to leave a message. "Hi, Sylvia, it's Ethan. Please call me as soon as you can. It doesn't matter what time of night or day it is. I need to talk to you urgently about Christopher. I hope to speak to you soon."

Ethan ended the call and rang Sylvia's mobile phone, but it went straight through to voicemail. Ethan left the same message he'd left on her answerphone at home and hung up.

He put his mobile phone on the coffee table and picked his laptop up. In many respects, he was relieved she hadn't answered so he didn't have to break the news to her that night. His conscious was also clear that he'd at least tried to call her.

As Ethan scrolled through his playlist of music, it occurred to him that he could do a quick *Google* search to find out what caused humans to foam at the mouth. He clicked on the internet icon and typed into the search bar *What causes humans to foam at the mouth?* Ethan's eyes widened, and his jaw dropped when he read that drug overdoses or rabies were the main causes.

To the best of his knowledge, Christopher hadn't been bitten by a rabid dog so that only left a drug overdose. But that didn't make any sense because Christopher had never taken drugs in his life. If he had, Ethan would have known about it.

Ethan took a sip of his drink and sat back in the chair. After a few minutes of reflective thought, he concluded that if Christopher had died of a drug overdose, then somebody must have doped him before or during the fight.

Ethan reached for his mobile phone and searched for the video he'd taken of the fight. He reached for his drink, drained the glass and waited for it to numb his senses a bit. When he pressed the play button, he was going to have to relive the nightmare he suspected would haunt him for the rest of his days and deal with all the emotions it was going to provoke. But he felt compelled to watch and study the video to see if there were any signs of somebody doping Christopher before or during the fight.

As he watched the video, Ethan made a mental note of Christopher drinking from the bottle Dan had handed him before the fight and the way he'd squirmed and pulled a face once he'd drunk whatever was in the bottle.

Ethan paused the video when Desmond the Destroyer had Christopher in a bear hug and was in close contact with him. He didn't see any visible signs of a needle or anything else in Desmond's hand so he pressed play again.

The only other person and opportunity would have been when Mike, the referee, grabbed Christopher from behind and pulled him away from Desmond the Destroyer when he was pulverising his face and head with his fists.

When the video reached the clip of Christopher running toward him and Dan, Ethan was about to stop the video but paused it when he saw what looked like the ghostly figure of a young man standing beside and slightly behind Christopher. He stared at the screen and focused on the man who was skeleton thin and had black, hollow eyes and a haunting face.

Ethan shivered, and the hairs on his arms stood on end. He looked at the screen again and knew his eyes weren't playing tricks on him. What he assumed was the ghost of a man who looked like he'd been tortured or had died of a drug overdose was standing beside Christopher.

The vision completely spooked Ethan out, and his scrambled brain couldn't make any sense of why he was there or if he was actually there. All he knew was something very strange was going on, and it was beyond his ability to make any sense of it.

Ethan took a sip of his drink and contemplated whether he should send the video to Dan. Then he reminded himself that Christopher had drunk from his bottle so Dan may have been the one who'd doped him. He tried to dismiss the idea because Dan had been like a father to Christopher so he struggled to imagine he'd have been capable of, or responsible for, causing Christopher any harm. It was far more likely that Desmond the Destroyer or Mike had reason to dope Christopher, so the fight was rigged.

The more Ethan thought about it, the more he decided that one of the three people who'd had access to Christopher before or during the fight had wanted to dope Christopher so he wouldn't win the fight. He suspected and hoped that whoever had done it probably hadn't intended to kill Christopher and had misjudged the dosage. Either way, he had to treat all three of them as potential suspects so he couldn't share the video footage with any of them.

Ethan's brain ached, and the veins in his temples pounded as he thought about Christopher's death, wondered if somebody had deliberately killed him, and if so, why they'd killed him. His heart ached knowing he'd never see Christopher alive again and that he faced a lonely and empty future without him.

Music had always been Ethan's saviour, and if there had ever been a time in his life when he needed to distract himself from the dark and troubling thoughts plaguing his mind, it was then. He knew he had to make an effort to instil some normality and sanity back into his life. He needed to feel Christopher's presence in one way or another to give him the strength to not go through with some of the crazy ideas and plans that were relentlessly running through his mind.

Ethan put his mobile phone down on the coffee table and picked up his laptop. He looked through the list of music he had and searched for a song that would offer him some comfort. He saw the title of *No Air* by Jordan Sparks featuring Chris Brown. His subconscious took control, and he clicked on it. As soon as the song started playing, Ethan took a deep breath and put his hands to his chest. The words were so relevant to how he felt. The thought of having to confront a future that didn't involve Christopher suffocated him.

Visions of Christopher flashed through Ethan's mind. He leaned forward, rested his elbows on his legs and massaged the bridge of his nose to help him relax and encourage his nasal passages to open so he'd be able to breathe more easily. His body was tense and rigid, and he feared it would give up on him and shut itself down if he didn't relax and slow his overactive mind down.

As the song came to an end, Ethan scrolled through the other music he had. When he saw *Fistful of Tears* by Maxwell, he instantly clicked on it. The song started playing, and Ethan listened to the words. He clenched his fists and banged them against his forehead. He wanted to beat out the thoughts, feelings, regrets, sadness, worry and self-pity that were trapped inside his head.

Ethan sat back in his chair and stared at the wooden slatted blinds covering the window—a blank canvass that gave him free rein and thought to unleash the beast lying in the depths of his subconscious.

The furnace inside him burned and the molten lava began to rise. Ethan shifted uncomfortably in his chair as he waited for the onslaught. He didn't know if he was going to throw his guts up or cry his eyes out again.

The burning sensation rose up from Ethan's stomach to his throat, and he breathed deeply through his nose and breathed out slowly through his mouth. After a while, the burning sensation subsided, and Ethan relaxed a bit.

As he looked around the room, Ethan caught a glimpse of

a photo of him and Christopher. Ethan covered his face with his hand to block out the vision of them together, but the sight of Christopher was ingrained in his mind.

It started with sniffles, but within seconds, Ethan's flood gates opened and the torrent of emotion he'd been doing his best to hold back flowed freely.

After a few minutes of intense crying and being plagued with thoughts of taking his own life so he could be with Christopher again and be free of the pain and suffering he was enduring, Ethan slapped himself around his face to try and bring himself back to his senses.

Ethan sat back in his chair, looked up to the sky, whaled and put his hands together in front of him in a praying position. He clapped his hands together and breathed in deeply. "I'm sorry, Christopher. I will get a grip of myself eventually. I just need some time. This is so hard for me, and I want to be with you so much it hurts."

Ethan was so wrapped up in his own drama and trauma that he was oblivious to everything else apart from his thoughts of Christopher. When *In My Blood* by Shawn Mendes started playing, Ethan's ears pricked up, and he sat upright in his chair. It was another one of Ethan and Christopher's favourite songs and Ethan was convinced Christopher was there with him in spirit, and the song was his way of telling him that the things he was thinking about weren't in his blood. That he was stronger than that, and he'd get by and be able to survive without him.

Sensing Christopher was there with him in spirit, Ethan went to the kitchen and poured himself another drink. He went back to the lounge, put his glass on the table beside his armchair, and went upstairs to the bedroom.

He opened the top drawer of his bedside cabinet and searched for the packet of sleeping tablets he kept there. He took one out of the packet, went back to the lounge and sat down in his armchair. He picked his drink up, took a swig, put the tablet in his mouth and swallowed it.

As the scotch and sleeping tablet started to take effect, Ethan's mind slowed down, and he felt lethargic. *Crush* by Yuna featuring Usher played in the background, and his thoughts were taken back to when he'd first met Christopher and the painfully beautiful crush he'd quickly developed for him. Ethan closed his eyes and visions of the videos he'd watched with Christopher flashed through his mind.

Ethan smiled as he visualised them walking along the beach front in Miami when they'd gone on holiday together for the first time. He'd felt so proud when they'd walked along holding hands and cuddling. At the time, he'd imagined he'd been the envy of every gay man who'd past them because Christopher had got looks of wanting desire from most of them.

A wave of emotion flowed from Ethan's throat to his stomach and then his crotch. He swallowed hard as he recalled the moment when they'd returned to the hotel room after their first day at the beach.

Christopher opened the door and entered the room, which was a lot cooler than the outside temperature courtesy of the air conditioning. Ethan followed him and closed the door behind him. Christopher stood in the middle of the room and pulled his vest top off. He turned around to face Ethan, and his swollen meat was visible through his thin nylon shorts. Ethan knew what he craved and was more than willing to oblige.

Ethan walked toward him. Christopher wrapped his arms around Ethan's lower back and pulled him closer. Ethan put his hands on Christopher's powerful shoulders and looked up at him. Christopher kissed him hard on the mouth, lowered his hands and caressed his firm backside. Ethan was powerless to resist his firm touch, his lips pressed against his and his hard tongue exploring his mouth. He curled his tongue and caressed Christopher's. He savoured his taste, the scent of suntan lotion, his warm skin pressed against his, his manly hands caressing his butt cheeks, and the feel of the gritty grains of sand that had stuck to his body.

Christopher put his hands on Ethan's vest top and lifted it over his head, threw it on the floor and winked at him. He mouthed *I want you. I want you bad.* Ethan gazed into his eyes and mouthed *I want you, and I want you now. I'm yours to take, so take me.*

With temperature and hormone levels rising, Christopher took hold of Ethan's hand and stuffed it inside his shorts. Ethan felt Christopher's long, hard shaft in his hand and teased it by gently gliding his hand along the length of it. Christopher gasped and blew out air. He covered Ethan's mouth with his and forcibly penetrated it with his tongue. He plunged his thick warm tongue in Ethan's mouth and pulled it back repeatedly while Ethan stroked and gripped his wanting shaft until he could feel the veins pulsating in his hand.

Christopher tipped his head back and looked down at Ethan. He blew out air and mouthed *Suck me.* Ethan kneeled on the floor. He tugged Christopher's shorts down, and his dick popped out and bounced in front of Ethan's face.

Once Ethan had pulled Christopher's shorts down to his ankles, he gripped the base of Christopher's cock, and a surge of blood turned the bulbous crown a reddish purple. Ethan swallowed to produce saliva, opened his mouth and welcomed Christopher's delicious meat into his mouth. He caressed the tip of Christopher's cock with his tongue, and when his mouth and throat were lubricated, he put a hand on Christopher's backside and applied pressure, inviting him to fuck his mouth and throat.

Christopher responded by slowly thrusting his groin

forward, and his dick slid further into Ethan's mouth. Ethan relaxed the muscles in his throat, and his throbbing cock glided to the back of it. Christopher groaned as Ethan sucked and rolled his tongue along his shaft, pulled his head back and pushed it forward so he could feast on Christopher's addictive cock.

While Ethan indulged himself in adoring Christopher's manly meat, he caressed his bulking muscular thighs and waves of pleasure rushed through his body. He'd always had a fetish for large thighs and butts so it heightened his euphoria to be touching what he considered to be his god. The man he worshipped and adored.

Christopher put his hands under Ethan's chin and pulled his cock out of his mouth. Ethan looked up at him, and Christopher winked. *Now I'm going to take you, baby,* he mouthed. He crouched down, put his hands under Ethan's armpits and pulled him up to his feet.

Ethan took Christopher's dick in his hand and stimulated it with his hand. Christopher put his hands on Ethan's butt cheeks and lifted him. Ethan instinctively wrapped his legs around Christopher's lower back and put a hand around the back of his neck. He let go of Christopher's throbbing cock and put his other hand to his mouth. He spat on his fingers and rubbed them against his pulsating hole.

Once he was satisfied he was ready to accept Christopher inside him, he put his hand in front of him and searched for Christopher's dick. When he had it in his hand, he guided it toward his open hole.

Ethan was so aroused and eager that he showed no resistance when Christopher's cock entered him. He released his grip on Christopher's dick and let him take control. He leaned forward and kissed Christopher passionately and lustfully.

Christopher responded by pulling Ethan toward him, and

his rigid cock penetrated the depths of Ethan's arse, stimulating his prostate gland. Ethan was overwhelmed with ecstatic pleasure, and he longed for Christopher to fuck him until his man pussy was wet and satisfied.

As Christopher used his manly hands and strength to lift Ethan up and lower him down, so his cock plunged in and out of Ethan's manhole, Ethan panted. Knowing his man was inside him and filling him up with his love and heated passion, Ethan gripped the back of Christopher's solid neck. His warm skin, solid muscles and rock-hard cock had never felt so good.

Ethan bounced up and down on Christopher's cock as he fucked him the way he knew he liked it—a bit rough, but never without feeling and passion.

The sweat rolled down Ethan's face and chest, and his hands slipped on Christopher's neck as the heat and passion rose, but it heightened his senses and pleasure.

Christopher repeatedly lifted Ethan up and let him slide down on his shaft that was wet with sweat and Ethan's love juices. When Christopher moaned and announced he was about to cum, Ethan gripped his own dick with his right hand and stimulated it. He looked at Christopher and just seeing his beautiful handsome face, feeling him inside him and knowing he was in contact with his colossal muscular body triggered a reaction. His balls tingled, and a euphoric sensation flowed along the length of his shaft to the crown of his dick.

Cum spurted out of Ethan's dick, and his body shuddered as the transparent liquid left his body and squirted all over Christopher's chest and stomach. Ethan exhaled when he squeezed the last drop out.

Ethan's orgasm had clearly pleased and excited Christopher because he pumped Ethan's arse harder. He released one hand from Ethan's arse and rubbed his hand on his chest and stomach. He leaned forward, moved the hand that was caressing Ethan's arse to his lower back.

As he cradled Ethan in his arm, he looked down at Ethan, exhaled sharply and pounded his arse. When the moaning and grunts got louder and faster, Ethan knew he was going to cum.

A few seconds later, Christopher looked at Ethan, and mouthed *Oh, baby, I'm gonna cum and fill you up with my love.* Ethan bit his lip and threw his head back while he waited to be filled up even more.

Ethan gasped for breath, sat upright and shook his head. He covered his mouth with his hands and blew out air. He looked around him, and he was still in his lounge, sat on his armchair. He closed his eyes and massaged his temples. Had he been dreaming? If he had, it had been the most vivid dream he'd ever had.

It had felt so nice and comforting to have been with Christopher again — to feel his touch, smell his unique scent, and make love to him, but after a few moments of reflective thought, Ethan surmised that he must have fallen asleep but was still half conscious and that was why the dream had seemed so real.

Once again, Ethan was consumed by a sense of emptiness and loneliness, and he wondered once again if he'd be reunited with Christopher if he took his own life. When the thought plagued his mind to the point of distraction, Ethan drained his glass and put himself to bed in the hope he'd sleep until the morning without any more disturbing thoughts.

CHAPTER THREE

With the help of the scotch and the sleeping tablet, Ethan managed to sleep for five hours. It was six in the morning when he woke up and even though he didn't want to wake up and confront the world, his nightmarish thoughts forced him to get out of bed. He went to the kitchen and put the kettle on so he could make himself a cup of tea. His stomach churned with nerves, and he felt sick. When he thought about what had happened to Christopher and how lonely he was going to be without him, Ethan started retching. He ran to the kitchen sink and leaned over it. His stomach muscles contracted, and his mouth was filled with acidic bile that he spat into the sink. Once his moment of anxiety had passed, Ethan went to the lounge and sat down on a chair while he tried to control his erratic breathing and calm himself down.

Ethan sat there staring at the television screen for what seemed like hours. He was oblivious to what he was watching because all he could think about was Christopher and what he should do next. The silence was broken by his mobile phone ringing. He looked at the screen and saw it was a call from Dan. He pressed the accept call button and held the phone to his ear.

"Hi, Ethan, I hope I didn't wake you up, but I've got some news for you from the pathologist."

"No. No, you didn't wake me up. So what has the pathologist said?"

"He said it's pretty clear Christopher died from a traumatic brain injury that must have been caused when Desmond the

29

Destroyer head butted him. As you saw, he took a really nasty blow to the head, and he was pretty shaken up by it."

"Yes, I saw that, and I'll never forget it for as long as I live. But that doesn't explain . . ."

"Explain what?"

Ethan paused and decided it was best not to say anything. "Nothing. Forget it. It was nothing. I'm afraid my head is all over the place right now."

"I can well imagine, but at least now we know what caused it. How are you coping?"

"Probably not the best question to ask me at the moment. I'm sitting here like a zombie, but I know I have to speak to Christopher's mother and start making the funeral arrangements. I just can't seem to force myself to think about it at the moment. I still can't accept that Christopher's dead, even though I witnessed it with my own eyes."

"Hey, give yourself some time. It came as a shock to all of us. Christopher was so young and healthy, and he seemed invincible, but unfortunately, that head butt proved to be too much for him. Look, if it'd help, I can make the funeral arrangements if it's too much for you to cope with at the moment. I think the sooner we bury Christopher, the sooner you'll be able to come to terms with your loss and start moving forward."

"That's very kind of you, Dan, but I think it's only appropriate that I make the arrangements. I want to give Christopher a very special send-off, and I want it to be a small and intimate affair—close friends and relatives only."

"That's your prerogative, and I'm sure you have a better idea than I do of what kind of send-off Christopher would have wanted. I don't want to put you under pressure or rush you, but we really should aim to arrange the funeral as soon as possible. I'm sure the people at the funeral directors will do their best to make him look the same way we remember him by, but his injuries were pretty bad, so the sooner, the better."

"Sure. I'll try and snap out of this trance and make a start today. Oh. Can you let me have the details of the undertaker and where his body is?"

"Sure. I'll send you a text as soon as we get off the phone."

"Thanks, Dan. I'll have to speak to Christopher's mother because if my memory serves me right, they have a family plot at West Norwood Cemetery. If I'm right, I'm pretty sure she'll want him to be buried there. Once I've spoken to her and confirmed where he's going to be buried, I'll let you and the funeral directors have the details of where it's going to be, the invitation list and where the wake will be held."

"Oh, right. So he's going to be buried and not cremated?"

"Yes. Why? Is there a problem with that?"

"Erm . . . no. It's just that burials seem a bit old-fashioned these days, that's all. I assumed he'd be cremated."

"Nope. He made it clear to me he wanted to be buried alongside his family and not cremated."

"Okay. Well, if there's anything I can do to help, you only have to let me know."

"I know, Dan, and thanks for all your support. I think I'm going to need all the support I can get over the next few days."

"Give yourself a bit of time, and I'm sure you'll be fine. You're probably a lot stronger than you think you are."

"Hmm. Let's hope you're right. Anyway, Dan, I suppose I'd better get my arse into gear and start doing something."

"No problem. I'll send you a text now."

"That's great. Bye for now, Dan."

Ethan hung up the phone and scratched his head. Either the pathologist had worked throughout the night to identify what had been the cause of Christopher's death or Dan was trying to palm him off with what sounded like the most likely and plausible cause.

Ethan couldn't get it out of his head that a traumatic brain injury was unlikely to have caused Christopher to foam at the mouth before he'd died. He reached for his laptop and did a search for symptoms of a traumatic brain injury. When he read one of the articles, he noted that while it could cause vomiting, there was no mention of foaming at the mouth. Neither did it explain why the ghostly figure who looked like he'd been drugged out of his mind was standing close to Christopher.

Everything seemed too convenient to be real, and Ethan's suspicion that something sinister had taken place before or during the fight continued to grow. He knew he wouldn't be able to settle or draw closure until he'd found out the truth. If it was proven that Christopher had died from a head injury, then he'd have to accept it, but the foaming at the mouth suggested that a head injury hadn't been the cause.

After some careful consideration, Ethan concluded that he couldn't and didn't want to go to the police. That would have caused too many complications and could have serious repercussions if Dan and the organisers of the illegal cage fights found out he'd gone to them. His only other option was to use the services of a private investigator.

As he leaned forward to pick his laptop up, his train of thought was broken by the sound of his mobile phone ringing. He looked at the screen, and it was Christopher's mother, Sylvia, calling him. He took a deep breath and braced himself. "Hi, Sylvia. I'm glad you've called me."

"Oh, darling, I'm so sorry I didn't call you sooner, but I went away on a spa weekend with a friend of mine, and I turned my mobile phone off because we were in such a remote place we had no signal. So tell me. What's happened to Christopher? Is he in trouble? Has he been arrested because he took part in the fight last night? What's happened?"

"Sylvia, I hate to break this news to you, but it's worse than anything else that could have happened."

"What? Is he seriously injured? Is he dead?"

"The latter, I'm afraid, Sylvia."

There was a momentary silence and Ethan could hear Sylvia breathing heavily and sobbing. "Please tell me it's not true. Tell me my baby boy isn't dead." Sylvia blew her nose, and her sobbing continued.

"Sylvia. I'm still in shock myself. I was there and witnessed it."

"No!"

The way Sylvia elongated the *no* reminded Ethan of a wolf howling in pain or sorrow and the hairs on his arms stood on end.

After a momentary pause, Sylvia cleared her throat. "So, it's true?" Sylvia made a strange noise, and to Ethan, it sounded as if she'd retched or choked on her words when she'd said them.

"I'm afraid so, Sylvia."

"Ethan, I'm really sorry, but I'll have to call you back. I'm having palpitations, and I can hardly breathe. I'll call you back once I've got a grip of myself."

"Okay, Sylvia, but please don't leave it too long, or I'll worry about you."

"Don't worry. I'll call you back as soon as I can, but I have to go now."

Sylvia hung up. Ethan put his mobile phone down, covered his face with his hands and breathed out heavily. He'd been dreading having to tell Sylvia, but he knew she had to know. He'd planned to break the news to her more gently, but what he'd planned to say and what spewed out of his mouth were two completely different things, and he felt awful for being so direct and to the point.

While he waited for Sylvia to call him back, Ethan paced around the living room and prayed she'd be okay. At her age, the shock of finding out her only son was dead could have been enough to kill her, and then he'd have felt responsible for her death as well as Christopher's.

Ethan walked to the bay window and looked outside. It was a beautiful late summer morning. The sun was shining, and the leaves on the trees swayed in the gentle breeze, creating their own enchanting form of ballet. He stared aimlessly at the cars and people that passed by and reminded himself that there was still life in the outside world, and that his life would go on, no matter what challenges Christopher's departure presented him with.

After a few minutes, Ethan turned around, looked at his mobile phone and willed it to ring. He waited another few minutes, and his nerves got the better of him. He walked to his mobile phone and sent Sylvia a text message asking her if she was okay.

He sat in the armchair, clutched his phone and stared at the screen. As he waited for it to beep or ring, he massaged the back of his neck with his free hand to try and relieve some of his tension.

After what seemed like an eternity, Ethan's mobile phone rang. He looked at the screen, and it was Sylvia calling him. He quickly pressed the accept call button. "Hi, Sylvia, are you okay?"

"Not really, but I'm hoping that once the anxiety tablet I've just taken has had its desired effect, I'll calm down a bit, and we'll be able to continue our conversation." Sylvia's voice wavered and cracked as she seemingly forced the words out. "I saw your text message, darling, but I had to have a good cry before I called you back. Ethan, I just can't get my head around the fact that my one and only son is dead. I never thought for a minute I'd have to bury my son. That's not the way it's meant to be! Your children are meant to outlive you. As soon as you told me, I could literally feel my heart break into two pieces, and I don't think it'll ever mend itself. I mean, how could it? This is a mother's worst nightmare—hearing that her son has died. I've always known there was a risk of it happening one day, but no . . . of course . . . I've always hidden and protected myself behind denial. I thought my Christopher was invincible, knew what he was doing, and that he'd never put himself in a life-threatening situation. I'm so damned frustrated he didn't listen to either of us. If he had, you and I wouldn't be having this dreadful conversation."

"I understand and completely empathise with you, Sylvia, but unfortunately, we both have to face up to reality right now."

"I know, darling, and I'll do my best to be as strong as I can while I'm on the phone to you. Whatever happens after that is anybody's guess, but hey ho. So tell me, how did he die? Was it during the fight?"

"Yes, it was during the fight. Christopher was head-butted, and the pathologist has said the blow was the cause of his death, but I have my doubts. I was about to phone a private investigation firm before you called because I'm struggling to believe it was the head butt that killed him."

Sylvia gasped and let out a yelp. "So what do you think did kill him?"

"It's probably best if I come over to your place later and show you the video I took of the fight, but in short, at the end of the fight, that Christopher won incidentally, he came running toward me and suddenly stopped in his tracks, reached for his throat and then started foaming at the mouth. Then he started vomiting, fell to the floor, and well . . . the rest, you know."

"Oh, my goodness. My poor baby. So what do you think caused that to happen?"

"I've been doing some research, and the most likely causes are rabies or a drug overdose."

"What?" Sylvia bellowed. "But Christopher has never

taken drugs in his life, and I can't imagine he'd been bitten by a rabid dog."

"My thoughts exactly, and that's why I want to contact a private investigation firm. I need to know what the cause of Christopher's death really was."

"I'm completely with you on that score. If foul play's involved, we need to know about it and make sure justice is served."

"Yes, and I know you probably don't want to think about this right now, but we need to make the funeral arrangements. Am I right in thinking you have a family plot at West Norwood Cemetery?"

"Yes, we do so I'll speak to them to find out when we can bury him there. That's where I want my baby boy laid to rest—with his grandparents, and one day I'll join them. And after what's happened to Christopher that'll probably be a lot sooner than I expected."

"That's great, Sylvia, and it will simplify things if you can take care of the burial arrangements. I'll deal with the rest of the funeral arrangements."

"Okay. Ethan, forgive me, but I need time for all this to sink in and do my best to come to terms with it. Why don't you come over later and we can talk about things in more detail. Right now, I think I need to go to bed and cry myself to sleep. Hopefully, I'll be a bit better when I see you later."

"Okay, Sylvia, but please don't take any more tablets or do anything stupid. We need each other for support to get through this."

"I'll do my best for your sake, Ethan, but if you weren't here, I might be inclined to do something stupid. Christopher meant everything to me. He was my only child and my rock, so I honestly don't know if and how I'm going to cope without him being here."

"Hey, neither do I, and that's why it's so important we

prop each other up and give each other strength. Look. I'll let you get some rest, and I'll come over to see you later. Okay?"

"Yes, that'd be great. Why don't you come over for dinner? I'm sure neither one of us will have much of an appetite, but we both have to try and eat something."

"That sounds like a good plan. I'll see you about six. Is that okay with you?"

"That's fine. I'll see you then."

Ethan ended the call and put his phone on the coffee table. He held his head in his hands and shook it. He was devastated, and he imagined Sylvia was going to be even more devastated than he was once the reality of Christopher's death had sunk in.

To distract himself from his worrying and haunting thoughts, Ethan picked his laptop up and did a search for private investigators in the London area. When the search results came back, he was particularly intrigued by the name and description of Apparition Intervention firm because they specialised in cases that involved the help of ghosts and spirits. Given that it looked as if a ghost was standing close to Christopher when he'd died, he decided they were probably the best firm to talk to.

He made a note of their telephone number and called them. He was greeted by a cheerful young lady called Martine. He briefly explained what had happened and what his suspicions were and she assured him she'd get one of the investigators to call him back once she'd spoken to the owner, Robert, who'd decide who was best to deal with his enquiry.

CHAPTER FOUR

Once Martine had put the phone down to Ethan, she peered across at Robert's glass-fronted office and saw he was alone. She stood up, walked toward the door and tapped on it. Robert looked up, and when he saw it was Martine, he beckoned her to enter. Martine sat down in front of Robert's desk and recounted the conversation she'd had with Ethan.

Robert sat back in his chair and cupped his hands behind his head. "Hmm. This sounds like it could be an interesting case—illegal cage fighting and the sight of an apparition. What's Jane working on at the moment? With her background and karate skills, she'd definitely be the best person to deal with it."

"Hmm. She's just started work on the McCarthy case, but I'm sure she wouldn't object to one of the others taking over if she knew she could get her hands on a meaty case that she could really add some value to."

"Yeah. I think you're right. I can see she's in the office so open the door and ask her to join us."

"No problem." Martine stood up, went to the door and opened it. "Jane, can you join us for a few minutes. We think we might have something interesting for you."

Jane turned around, looked at Martine and held her hands out to the side. "But I'm working on the McCarthy case."

"We know, but we think you might be more interested in this one."

Jane cocked her head to the side and squinted. "Ooh. Sounds interesting. Give me a minute, and I'll be right with you."

Once Robert and Martine had briefed Jane on the potential new case, she leaned back in her chair and smiled. "Oh, yes. This definitely sounds right up my street." She looked at Robert. "I'll leave it up to you to reassign the McCarthy case to somebody else, shall I?"

"Yeah, no problem. Martine and I will work that out, and you can brief whoever I hand it over to."

"Great. So all I need now is the telephone number for Ethan, and I'll get cracking on this one. It sounds like it could be a lot of fun."

Robert chuckled. "More like dangerous fun, so make sure you're careful. I don't want you getting into any more scraps."

Jane laughed. "And what makes you think that I'd do that?"

Robert waved the back of his hand at Jane. "I know you all too well. Go and do a good job and just try to stay out of trouble."

"I'll do my best, but I can't make any promises. Right. Come on, Martine. Let me have Ethan's number, and I'll give him a call."

"Cool. Let's go."

Martine gave Jane the telephone number for Ethan, and she went to her desk.

Jane called Ethan, and after a few rings, the call connected. "Hello, Ethan. This is Jane from the Apparition Intervention team."

"Oh, hello, Jane. Thanks for calling me so soon."

"That's not a problem. I've been fully briefed by Martine and the owner of Apparition Intervention, so I'm calling to confirm how we move things forward."

"That's good to hear. Do you think you'll be able to help me get to the bottom of what happened to Christopher? Because I'm not convinced that Dan has told me the truth."

"Well, I think the appearance of the apparition in the video suggests something strange and untoward has gone on, but I'll have a better idea once I've seen the video footage."

"Okay. I live in South Norwood, in London, so how soon we will be able to meet?"

"Erm . . . I can pass by your house within an hour if that suits you?"

"It certainly does, and the sooner you can start looking into the case, the better because I'm sure that people will start putting me under pressure to arrange the funeral—especially the person or people who are responsible for Christopher's death."

"I agree. Can you let me have your address, please?"

Ethan told Jane where he lived, and she made a note of his address. She ended the call, grabbed her handbag, and walked toward the exit door. She turned to Martine. "I'm off to see Ethan. I'll call you or Robert later to let one of you know what I've found out."

Martine smiled and saluted her.

Once she'd got out of central London, the roads were a lot clearer although she did get stuck in some minor traffic jams in some of the smaller towns and main roads. When she arrived at Ethan's house, it was a pretty standard terraced house with a bay window upstairs and downstairs and a window above the door. Given Christopher had been a cage fighter, she'd expected the house to be a bit more glamorous—maybe a detached house with a swimming pool—but she had no real idea how much prize fighters won when they competed.

Jane knocked on the door, and within a few seconds, an attractive man in his mid-twenties, with an athletic build opened the door. Jane smiled and put her hand out to shake his. "Hi. I'm assuming you're Ethan?"

"Yes, that's right. Please come in, Jane, and thanks once again for coming to see me so soon."

Jane stepped into the hallway and waited for Ethan to close the door behind her and lead the way. Ethan walked in front of Jane and turned back to look at her. "Would you like a cup of tea or coffee?"

"A coffee would be nice if it's not too much trouble."

"Not at all. In that case, I think it's best if we go through to the kitchen diner and you can have a look at the video while I'm making the coffee."

Ethan led them through to the spacious kitchen diner which benefited from views of the pristine garden which had a recently mowed lawn and strategically placed flower beds that blossomed with vibrant and assorted late summertime colours. The rockery and water feature offered a welcomed sense of peace and relaxation, and the large hanging willow tree at the end of the garden added an element of mystery to the small suburban oasis.

Ethan pointed at the kitchen table. "Please take a seat. I'll put the kettle on, and then I'll go and get my mobile phone from the lounge."

Jane nodded and smiled. "That's fine. Take your time."

Ethan filled the kettle and switched it on. He walked past Jane and toward the hallway. While he was gone, Jane gazed out at the garden and decided she and her husband really ought to spruce their garden up a bit because it looked drab and shabby in comparison to Ethan's.

Ethan walked back into the kitchen and handed Jane his phone. "Just press play, and you'll be able to watch the video. I'll get the coffee sorted out." Ethan looked at Jane and winced. "I'd rather not watch it again, if that's all right with you?"

Jane nodded her head gently. "That's fine. If I've got any questions after I've watched it, I'll let you know." Jane pressed play and watched the video. She noted all the people Ethan suspected might have been responsible for doping Christopher. At the end, when she saw him grab his neck and start foaming at the mouth, she was pretty convinced that Ethan's suspicions had been right. Jane looked up, and Ethan was standing by the kitchen counter with two glass cups in his hands that were filled with coffee.

"So what do you think, Jane? Do you think Christopher was killed by a head injury, or do you think he was doped?"

"Hmm. Without tests being done, it's too early to say, but my experience and instincts tell me that he was doped. And the apparition of the guy who's standing by him definitely looks like a druggy, so that adds even more weight to that assumption as far as I'm concerned. Apparitions don't normally appear without a reason, and I'm guessing he wanted to help Christopher or at least he felt sorry for him because perhaps he'd been through the same horrid experience when he'd been on this Earth."

Ethan nodded and grimaced. "So what should we do? I don't want to make Dan suspicious I suspect him or the other two guys who were in the ring of doping Christopher or my life could also be in danger."

"No, don't say anything to anyone at the moment. The first thing we need to do is recover Christopher's body so a proper autopsy can be carried out. Hopefully, that'll give us a better insight into what really happened to him, and then I'll have more to work on."

"I agree. But I'm still waiting for Dan to let me have the details of where his body is. He said he was going to send me a text message when I spoke to him this morning, but I still haven't received it. And even when I do know where it is, how can we recover the body without Dan becoming suspicious? He arranged for an undertaker to collect the body from the warehouse and the so-called autopsy to be done. If we arrange for the body to be taken somewhere else, he's probably going to suspect something."

"That's a good point. What I'd suggest is you call Dan and tell him you want to see a copy of the autopsy report. I don't think he'll suspect anything from that. It's pretty normal for the bereaved to want to read it. Then tell him you want to go and see the undertakers to drop off the clothes you want Christopher buried in, and you want to see Christopher while you're there. If you think you can pull it off, tell him you want to go with me because we'll need a blood sample to find out if there are opioids in Christopher's blood. You can pretend I'm one of Christopher's close relatives or something. But if you'd rather go on your own and think you'll be able to take a blood sample that's fine, but I'd rather go with you, if that's possible."

"Hmm. I think it might be better if I go on my own. If I'm on my own, Dan won't suspect anything, and I'm sure he'll respect my request and wishes to be left alone with Christopher for a while. If you're with me, he's likely to insist on staying with us, and he'll be watching us, especially you, like a hawk."

"That's fine. Whatever you think's best, but you ideally need to do it today. If it's shown that Christopher was doped, then we need to act fast before Dan, or somebody else suspects something and decides to dispose of his body and the evidence they've left behind."

"I'll be able to take a blood sample. That won't be a problem."

"Okay. The most common place to take a blood sample from a corpse is the femoral veins or arteries which both run from the abdomen down to the thigh and then the rest of the leg. Given that Christopher hasn't been dead for that long and he was so fit, I'm sure you won't have a problem locating one of them, especially in his thigh, so you can draw the blood sample."

"Okay. Got it."

"Great. So we need to meet up afterwards so you can let me have the blood sample. Then I'll arrange for it to be tested and we should have the results back by the end of the day. Once we've got those, I'll decide what the next steps are. My main concern, for now, is that we get that blood sample."

"Okay. Once you've left, I'll call Dan and make the arrangements. I think I'll wait until I've got the blood sample before I ask him for the autopsy report. I don't want to trigger off any alarm bells, and if I ask him for the autopsy report now, it might just do that."

"You know him better than I do, so do what you think is right. If I let you have my mobile phone number could you send me the video footage of Christopher because I want to watch it on a big screen? Then, once you've got the blood sample, give me a call so we can arrange to meet up."

"Sure." Ethan walked to one of the kitchen units and took out a pen and notepad from one of the drawers. He walked back to the table and placed them in front of Jane. "Write the number down, and I'll store it in my phone."

Jane wrote her number down on the pad and stood up. "Right. I hope everything goes to plan and I'll see you later. If you have any problems with Dan, please be sure to give me a call."

"I will do, Jane. I'll be in touch later."

Ethan led the way to the street door and said goodbye to Jane as she left. As she walked toward her car, Jane planned what calls she had to make to ensure the blood tests would be completed that day. When she got into her car, she put her mobile phone in the hands-free cradle, put the key in the ignition and turned the engine on.

As Jane was driving home, her phone rang. She looked at the screen and didn't recognise the number. She connected the call. "Hello, Jane, here. Who is it?"

"Hi, Jane, it's Ethan. I'm sorry to trouble you, but I've just got off the phone to Dan, and I don't know . . . it was weird."

"Hi, Ethan. In what way was it weird?"

"Well, when he answered my call, I heard someone in the background say *wasn't the plan*. I think Dan covered the mouthpiece with his hand, but I faintly heard him tell whoever had said it to shut up."

"Okay. That could be interesting. Did you recognise the voice?"

"No. It was a man's voice, but not one I recognised."

"What happened after that?"

"I told him I wanted to go and see Christopher and asked him to let me know where his body was because I hadn't received his text message. He didn't say anything for a couple of seconds and then apologised for not sending the message and explained he was having a pretty frantic day. I told him I felt the need to see Christopher and wanted to take his clothes for the funeral to the undertakers so they could dress him. Without hesitation, he tried to put me off because he wasn't sure if the undertakers had, as he put it, cleaned him up."

"Has he sent you the text message with the details of the undertakers?"

"He has now, but only because I insisted. He seemed very reluctant to let me have their details and justified it with the reasoning that it could cause me even more distress if I saw Christopher before he'd been cleaned up."

"Okay. I can understand where he's coming from, but it does sound like he's trying to hide something. Is he going to meet you there?"

"Yes. He's going to meet me there, but I told him I wanted

some time with Christopher on my own and he said he'd respect my wishes."

"Okay. That's good. What about a syringe? Do you have any? If not, you should be able to buy one in a chemist. You might have to try a few, but I know some chemists sell them."

"That's fine. I'll go to our local chemist. I've been there enough times to get prescription pain killers and medicines for Christopher in the past, so they know me and won't have a problem letting me have a syringe."

"Excellent. Are you okay meeting up with Dan on your own? If you let me have the undertakers address, I can drive there and keep an eye on you from a safe distance."

"That's very kind of you, but I think I'll be all right. Even if Dan did have something to do with Christopher's death, I don't think he'll want another dead body on his hands. I'll send you the address though just in case I don't call you later. At least then, you'll know where to start looking for me."

"Yes, please do . . . and the video footage. When are you leaving to go to the undertakers?"

"I'm going to have a quick shower, shave, and get dressed, and then I'll be making a move. By the time I've been to the chemist, I should arrive at the undertakers in about ten minutes because it's pretty close to me."

"Okay. I'm on my way home because it's closer to your place than the office, so give me a call when you leave the undertakers, and I'll meet you at your place. If in the meantime, you need help, then give me a call, if you can, of course."

"Sure. I'm sure I'll be fine, but it's reassuring to know that I've got back up if I need it."

"You certainly do. Okay. I'll catch up with you later, and I look forward to getting your messages with the video and address of the undertakers."

"No problem. I'll send the messages before I get showered."

Jane disconnected the call and focused on the road ahead. After a minute, her phone beeped to notify her she'd received a message. About thirty seconds after that, it beeped again, and she was pretty certain they were the messages from Ethan.

When Jane arrived home, she went to her desk and looked at the messages she'd received. She scribbled the details of the undertakers in her notepad and then copied the video footage onto the hard drive of her computer. She clicked on the video and started watching it.

Jane observed that after Christopher had drunk from the bottle Dan had given him, he pulled a face which might have indicated that the water or whatever was in the bottle, tasted strange and could have contained opioids.

As Desmond stood in front of Christopher, Jane studied his hands, feet and boxer shorts, but couldn't see any signs of how he might have been able to dope Christopher. Everything looked clean, and she was mystified. Her only hope was that she'd notice something when the referee grabbed him from behind.

Jane cringed when she saw the pain Christopher had been in when Desmond had him in a bear hug, and head-butted him. Christopher looked visibly stunned and dazed. After Christopher head-butted Desmond's nose and kneed him in the crotch, and Desmond released his grip on Christopher and stepped back the video froze, but Jane hadn't pressed the pause button.

Instinctively, Jane suspected it had happened for a reason and that she might not have been alone. She looked at the still shot, but couldn't see anything unusual, so she pressed play again. The video played for a few seconds, and without her touching anything, the video rewound to the image of Desmond that she'd previously looked at.

Jane looked to her left and saw nothing. She turned to her right, and the apparition of the man in the video was standing beside her. She smiled at him. "Hi. Thanks for stopping by. I take it you're here because you want to point out something I've missed?"

The man looked at Jane. His face was expressionless, and his eyes were hauntingly dark and hollow. He nodded and leaned forward. He pointed to the wide elasticated waistband on Desmond's red silk shorts. Jane zoomed in on the waistband and gasped when she saw three tiny needle tips poking out.

She turned to look at the apparition so she could thank him, but he'd disappeared. Jane took a screenshot of Desmond's waistband and saved it on her computer. She sat back in her chair and blew out air. The tiny needles almost confirmed that Christopher had been doped, but until she had the results of the blood sample, she wouldn't know for sure.

Jane contemplated calling Ethan to let him know what she'd discovered but decided it would be better to tell him in person after he'd left the undertakers with the blood sample. If she told him before, she feared it might push him over the edge, and he might jump to conclusions about who'd been responsible for killing Christopher. Worse still, he might have told Dan, and she didn't want him to do that—not until she'd had the opportunity to interview the three suspects.

Jane printed out the photo of Desmond's waistband, which clearly showed the small needles poking out of it so she could show it to Ethan when she saw him. Then she called the laboratory the Apparition Intervention team frequently used to let them know she'd be arranging for a blood sample to be sent to them. She emphasised that their first priority was to check for traces of opioids. They assured her that if she got the sample to them by four that afternoon, they'd have the results back to her by six.

Suspecting Ethan would be calling her in a couple of hours, Jane made herself an early lunch. She had no idea what time she'd get back from Ethan's so she decided it was prudent to have something to eat before she left.

CHAPTER FIVE

As Ethan approached the funeral director's office, which was located on a main road a couple of miles from where he lived, he saw Dan standing outside pacing backward and forward. He beeped his horn to attract his attention and Dan leaned forward and held his right hand out to acknowledge he'd see him. Ethan waved and drove on. When he saw a side street on his left, he indicated to turn left. He hoped he might find a parking space somewhere off the main road. Once he'd parked his car, he grabbed the bag that he'd packed Christopher's clothes in, got out, locked his car and walked toward the funeral home.

As he turned right into the main road, Etan's head was awash with mixed emotions. He knew he wanted to see Christopher again, but his sorrow, grief and anger rapidly rose with every step he took.

Ethan talked to himself to try and momentarily force his thoughts to the back of his mind so he'd calm down. He had to focus on the task at hand and not give Dan any reason to suspect he suspected him of killing Christopher.

When he reached Dan, Ethan stopped and held out his hand to shake Dan's. Once they had, Dan patted Ethan on his back and started walking toward the entrance of the funeral director's office. Ethan walked beside him, and the lump in his throat was harder to swallow, and he feared it might choke him.

When they entered, the undertaker who Ethan had previously met at the warehouse remained seated and indicated for them to both take a seat in front of his desk.

"Hello, Ethan. I'm sorry to be meeting you again in such sad circumstances, but you can rest assured that Christopher will be treated with dignity and respect while he's here with us. Before we move on, first things first. Let me give you the death certificate. You'll need that to register the death. If you don't do that you won't be able to bury Christopher." The undertaker reached into the top drawer of his desk, took out an A4 envelope and handed it to Ethan.

Ethan opened the envelope and took the death certificate out to check that all the details were correct, and he noted that the cause of death was shown as a fatal blow to the head. Ethan swallowed hard and cleared his throat. "Thank you. I'll pass it onto Christopher's mother. I guess she's the best person to register the death given she'll be making the arrangements for the funeral."

"In that case, it's best you let her have it. Okay, so given you've come to see him at such short notice, I'm afraid we haven't had time to fully prepare him for his burial and Dan mentioned earlier that you'd be bringing the clothes you want him buried in."

"Thank you. That means a lot to me, and yes, I have the clothes here in a bag." Ethan picked the bag up and handed it to the undertaker who put it down on the floor beside his desk.

"Excellent. Dan informs me you want the funeral arranged within the next few days. Is that correct?"

"Yes, Dan thought it'd be better if the funeral was arranged as soon as possible, given the circumstances."

"Yes, I agree. Do you have any idea of what kind of funeral you want for Christopher and where it will be?"

"Yes, he'll be buried in a family plot at West Norwood Cemetery, which is only a few miles away from where Christopher's mother lives. I'm afraid at this point the only other thing I know is that he wanted to be taken to his place of rest in a horse-drawn carriage. Can you arrange that?"

"That shouldn't be a problem. I have a few contacts who I'm sure can help me out to make sure we can accommodate Christopher's wishes."

"I've spoken to Christopher's mother, and she's assured me that she'll contact the cemetery today to make the arrangements so I should be able to let you know when it will be later on today. She sort of knows them from past experiences, and if anyone can sweet talk them into arranging the burial at such short notice, it'll be her. As soon as I've got the date and time, I'll give you a call."

"That's great. I'm assuming the funeral procession will be leaving from Christopher's mother's house?"

"I haven't confirmed it with her yet, but that would be the obvious choice given she lives near Brockwell Park Gardens, and it's a lot closer to the cemetery than I am. I'm seeing her later tonight so that'll be another thing I'll confirm with you in the morning. If we agree the procession will leave from her house, I'll let you have her address."

"That's fine, and I know Brockwell Park Gardens fairly well. Okay, well I'm afraid Christopher is still in the morgue, so it's going to be a bit more distressing to see him there as opposed to seeing him in the chapel of rest when he's dressed, and we've managed to properly prepare him for his funeral."

"I fully understand, and Dan already forewarned me. Just one last question and I apologise in advance for sounding so ignorant, but how many mourners can travel in each limousine?"

"Hmm, in theory, they can hold seven to nine people but to make things more comfortable, I'd limit the number to six in each car."

"Okay, once I've confirmed the invitation list, I'll let you know how many cars we need."

"That's not a problem. We don't have that much on this week, so there shouldn't be a problem. Okay, before we go through, I just wanted to let you know that given the funeral will be arranged quickly, if you choose the coffin you want for him today, we'll have him ready and in his coffin in the chapel of rest first thing tomorrow morning. So if you want to come back and see him again after nine that won't be a problem."

"Okay. Can you show me the collection of coffins you have available so I can choose one now? I'd rather get that over and done with before I see Christopher."

"Of course, but given the intention is to bury Christopher at short notice, I'm afraid you'll have to choose a coffin from the limited stock we have available here. Unfortunately, there won't be time to have a tailor-made coffin prepared."

"That's fine. Christopher didn't have any specific requests about the coffin he's buried in, so I'm sure I'll find something I like from the range you've got here. Shall we have a look at them now so we can get that out the way?"

"Sure. If you'd like to follow me, I'll show you what we can offer you." The undertaker stood up and started walking toward a door to his left. Ethan and Dan stood up and followed him. The undertaker opened the door and indicated that Ethan and Dan should enter.

They walked into the large rectangular room where each coffin was displayed on top of two solid dark wooden blocks. Ethan stopped and looked around the room. His blood turned cold, and he was overwhelmed with an uncontrollable desire to throw up. He'd never envisaged having to choose a coffin for Christopher at such a young age, and he didn't like being in a room that surrounded and suffocated him with thoughts of death and sorrow.

Dan put a hand on Ethan's shoulder. "Come on. Let's choose a coffin as fast as we can so we can get out of this room.

It makes me shudder just being in here."

"Well, that makes two of us. Let's go and have a look at them and choose one between us."

They slowly walked around the perimeter of the room and studied each coffin in turn. They both made comments about what they liked and didn't like about each one—the colour, design, fittings, and most importantly, if they thought it was fitting for Christopher's final resting place.

After a few minutes of deliberation, Ethan and Dan both agreed on the *Marlborough* coffin that was oak veneer with a walnut stain. The brass handles and fittings looked elegant, but manly, and Ethan was confident it would get Sylvia's seal of approval.

Ethan and Dan left the display room and joined the undertaker at his desk. Ethan sat down and looked at the undertaker. "We've decided on the *Marlborough* coffin with the walnut stain."

The undertaker nodded. "An excellent choice. Once you've seen Christopher, we'll start work on getting him ready for the chapel of rest so you'll be able to come and see him again tomorrow if you want to and he'll look more like his old self, and he'll be in more pleasant surroundings."

"That's great, thank you. I definitely want to see him again before he's laid to rest." Ethan could feel the tears starting to well up in his eyes, and he wanted to be with Christopher while he was on his own so that nobody else would witness his breakdown. "Okay, so if there's nothing more for us to discuss at the moment, would it be possible to see Christopher now?"

The undertaker stood up and gestured with his hand to follow him. "Please, come with me."

Ethan and Dan stood up and started to follow the undertaker. Ethan looked across at Dan and put an arm on his forearm. "Dan, as I said on the phone, I want to be with

Christopher on my own. I can sense I'm going to get very emotional and I don't want anybody being there with me to witness it. If you want to see him after I've left, that's fine, but please respect my wishes."

"Dan stopped in his tracks. "Of course. That's fine. I've already seen him because I got here a little bit early and I'll come back tomorrow to see him again. I'll just wait for you outside."

"Really, Dan, there's no need. I'll be fine, and to be honest, I could be in there for hours the way I feel at the moment. Go home, and I'll see you at the funeral. What time are you thinking of coming tomorrow?"

"Probably late afternoon. I've got some things I need to sort out in the morning."

"That's fine. I'll come here in the morning for a few hours. I'll be in touch with you as soon as I can to confirm the details of the funeral arrangements. In the meanwhile, would you e-mail me a copy of the autopsy report and the full names and telephone numbers for Mike and Desmond?"

"Yeah, sure, but if you want, I can call them if you're not up to it."

"Thanks, but I think it'll be better if I call them. I'm sure Desmond feels guilty and responsible for what's happened, so I think there's more chance of him coming to the funeral if the invitation comes from me. That way, he'll hopefully feel I don't hold him personally responsible."

Dan looked down at the floor and covered his mouth with his hand momentarily. "Sure, you're probably right. I'll send everything through to you when I get home."

"Thanks, Dan." Ethan looked toward the undertaker. "My apologies. We just had to talk about a few things."

"That's fine. Are you ready now?"

"Yes."

The undertaker led them through a corridor toward a door

on the left. He opened the door and gestured that Ethan should enter. Even though the temperature of the room hadn't dropped much the blood running through Ethan's veins chilled and he shivered. He'd never been in a morgue before, and it was heartbreaking to know that Christopher was lying in one of the cold stainless-steel chambers that were stacked two high and stretched the whole width of the room. Ethan scanned the ten chambers with his eyes and wondered which one his poor Christopher was lying in, cold, lonely and dead.

Ethan stood just inside the doorway almost paralysed as he watched the undertaker walk to the left-hand side of the room and stop at the third column of chambers. He crouched down and grabbed the handle with both hands and started walking backward. Ethan stared at the chamber and no matter how hard or often he swallowed the lump in his throat wouldn't go away.

Once the chamber was fully opened, the undertaker pulled down the plastic covering Christopher slightly. He turned to Ethan and walked toward him. "I'll leave you with Christopher now. I appreciate you want to see Christopher, but can I suggest you keep your visit fairly brief. Once he's in the chapel of rest, you can spend as much time as you want with him, but we need to make a start on getting him ready for the chapel of rest as soon as possible. I'm sure you understand."

Ethan nodded and started walking toward the open chamber. Visions of Christopher when he was alive flashed through his mind, and he knew he had to brace himself to see Christopher dead, covered in a plastic sheet and lying inside a metal chamber. He paused, looked up to the sky and crossed himself. "Please, God, give me the strength to be able to cope with this."

Once he'd drawn on all the inner strength he could muster up, he continued to walk, and Christopher's face came into view. Ethan covered his mouth, and warm tears began to stream down his face. He stood by the side of the chamber, then sat down with his back to the bank of chambers so he was facing Christopher and could see his face.

It looked as if the undertaker had applied some make-up to Christopher's face to try and mask some of the bruising, but it still had a whitish and yellow tinge to it. His only hope was that they'd done a quick job and that he'd look a lot more like the old Christopher he remembered when he was in the chapel of rest.

Ethan placed his right hand on the side of Christopher's head and winced. It all seemed so real and ugly feeling his cold and lifeless face. "Oh, my darling, you have been my superhero from the day I met you, and you have no idea how I wish we could have grown old together, shared an undying love, and do all the things we spoke about and planned to do. I can't believe I'm having to say goodbye to you at such a young age, but you'll forever be in my heart and mind. Nothing can take that away from me. Only death, but then I hope we meet again one day in Heaven, and we can live the life we'd always planned and be eternally happy."

As Ethan stroked Christopher's face and rocked backward and forward, he questioned if there really was a Heaven, or whether it was something that had been made up centuries ago to give people hope that they hadn't really lost their loved ones and would be reunited with them again. All he could do was pray that it really did exist and that he and Christopher would be together again one day.

"My darling. The memories I have of being with you will stay with me forever, so you'll always be a part of my life. I love you now as much as I did when we first met, and that will never change. I'll do whatever I can to make sure your mother is taken good care of, and try to be the son and role model you were to her, so she doesn't feel as if she's entirely lost her son. I know it's not much of a consolation for her, but hopefully, I'll be able to offer her some support and comfort."

Unaware of how long he'd been in the morgue, Ethan heard the door click. The undertaker poked his head around the door and looked at Ethan. "I'm really sorry to rush you, Ethan, but we have work to do in here, so could I ask you to say your goodbyes and leave in the next ten minutes? I feel awful asking you, but you'll be able to spend more time with him when he's in the chapel of rest."

"Yes, of course, I'm sorry. I completely lost track of time. Give me ten minutes, and I'll make a move."

"That's great, and thank you." The undertaker shut the door.

"Right, the love of my life, I have to leave shortly, but there's one little thing I have to do before I go. This won't hurt, and I know you'd thank me if you could because this is going to tell us exactly what happened to you and help us find the person or people who killed you."

Ethan pushed back the plastic sheet to expose Christopher's left thigh. It wasn't hard to spot the femoral veins because he'd been so muscly when he'd been alive. Ethan reached into his satchel and took out the cleaning agent the chemist had recommended and the bag of cotton gauze. He cleaned the area, took the needle and syringe out of his satchel and took the plastic protector cap off.

Despite his hand shaking slightly, he managed to prick the skin and started to slowly draw blood. Once the syringe was full, he carefully withdrew the needle and quickly replaced the protective cap.

Recalling his own experiences of having had blood tests, he pressed a clean piece of cotton gauze he had in his left hand against the puncture hole for about five minutes to ensure that no more blood came out and the vein didn't rupture. Using his right hand, he put the syringe in a narrow compartment in his satchel, making sure that the needle end was upright so there'd be no spillage or leaks.

He looked at Christopher, and as much as he wanted to kiss him on the lips, it didn't strike him as being appropriate, and he feared he'd get too emotional if he did. Instead, he kissed his fingers and placed them on Christopher's mouth. "Goodbye until tomorrow, my darling. I love you with all my heart, and that will never change. Even though you won't be here in a physical presence."

Content that he'd seen Christopher, had a good chat and cry with him, and he had the blood sample, Ethan stood up and closed the chamber. As he walked away, he desperately wanted to look back and wave goodbye, but he forced himself not to. He suspected he was going to have nightmares about his experience at the morgue for the rest of his life and it pained him so much to know Christopher was there surrounded by other dead bodies.

Ethan left the room and walked along the corridor to the undertaker's office, and his cheeks burned slightly. He hoped his face didn't give away the secret he was hiding. When he looked around the room, he was relieved Dan wasn't still there. That gave him one less thing to worry about.

He stopped in front of the undertaker's desk. "Thank you for everything, and letting me see Christopher. I'll be back here tomorrow at about ten, if that's okay with you?"

The undertaker nodded. "That's absolutely fine, Ethan. I'll make sure that Christopher is in the chapel of rest, and ready to receive you before you arrive. Goodbye for now, and I'll see you again tomorrow."

Ethan raised a hand. "Bye."

Once Ethan was safely in his car, he took out his mobile phone and called Jane. After a few rings, the call connected.

"Hi, Ethan. How did it go?"

"Hmm. A bit strange and very emotional, but I've got the blood sample and managed to get out of there in one piece."

"So, Dan didn't give you a hard time?"

"Not as such. He seemed a bit jittery and concerned, but he left me alone, so I could spend some time with Christopher."

"Okay. That's great. Listen, I've looked at the video again and discovered something very interesting that I'd like to show you. What time will you be back at home?"

"Erm. It should only take me ten to fifteen minutes to get back. Is it something you can tell me over the phone? After seeing Christopher, I feel more desperate than ever to find out what happened to him because apart from some bruising on his head that's been covered up with make-up, I'm still not convinced a head injury was the cause of his death."

"Look. I could, Ethan, but I'd rather tell you and show you what I've discovered in person. If it puts your mind at rest, I don't think a head injury was the cause of Christopher's death. I'll meet you at your place at about two-thirty, and I'll explain everything."

"Well, this is all sounding very ominous, but I'm pleased to hear that my suspicions could be right and I hope that what you've discovered will lead us to find out what really happened to Christopher and what caused his death."

"I'm hoping that what I've discovered and the results of the blood test will confirm my theory."

"Okay. I'm going to make my way back now, so make your way over as soon as you can."

"Great. I'll see you soon."

Ethan started the engine and put the car into gear. As he looked in his rearview mirror and the wing mirror, Ethan's mind was plagued with visions of Christopher lying in the metal chamber. He took the car out of gear and reached into the glove compartment to find the case of CDs. He flicked through them and put on a compilation CD he'd made for him and Christopher. He hoped it would remind him of the wonderful life he'd had with Christopher and distract him from the agonising visions that were flashing through his mind.

The first song that played was *2 Become 1* by the Spice Girls. It instantly reminded Ethan of the day when they'd first met and how quickly they'd fallen in love. Feeling a bit more relaxed with pleasant thoughts running through his mind, Ethan pulled away and started to drive home.

As he drove, and the words penetrated his mind, Ethan's thoughts were taken back to why the record meant so much to him. Christopher had played it to him after their first argument, and Ethan thought he was going to lose him. They'd argued over something that in retrospect seemed trivial. It mainly revolved around Christopher's struggle to accept his sexuality and the compromises Ethan had to make and obstacles he had to overcome to convince Christopher it was okay to be gay, and he didn't have to uphold his macho male image just to keep his family and friends happy.

At the beginning of their relationship, Christopher often got frustrated with Ethan because he didn't feel he understood the difficult situation he was in. He feared that once people on the cage fighting scene knew he was gay and with Ethan, he'd be mocked and ridiculed by everybody he knew.

It took months of patience and persistence on Ethan's behalf to gain Christopher's trust and give him the strength to confront his inner demons. Just thinking about the first few months of their relationship, Ethan was reminded of the song, *It's Impossible* by Christina Aguilera. Ethan had listened to it repeatedly when he'd been on his own because he could relate to the lyrics so much.

Initially, Christopher had made it impossible for Ethan to truly love him because he lived in fear of Christopher not being able to confront his own paranoia about his true sexu-ality and the people who he'd feared would reject him when they found out.

Slowly but surely, with the help of Ethan and Sylvia, Chris-topher made the decision that he wanted to live his life how he wanted to so he no longer had to lie to himself and deny himself the love Ethan had offered him, even if it meant losing some friends and having to give up the cage fighting.

Sylvia not only encouraged him to live his life how he'd wanted to, but she'd also have been elated if Christopher had walked away from the cage fighting scene. Ethan sighed. If she'd won her battle, Christopher would have still been alive and sharing his life and love with them.

To change his train of thought that was taking him down a helter-skelter, to God only knew where, at an alarmingly fast rate, Ethan played *Better With Time* by Leona Lewis. It gave him some comfort thinking things would get better with time, providing he drew on the inner strength he knew he had somewhere inside him, and clung onto his memories of Chris-topher and never lost the love he had for him.

CHAPTER SIX

When Jane arrived at Ethan's house, she knocked on the door, and he quickly opened it. His eyes were red and puffy, and Jane could only imagine what heartache and suffering he was going through. Ethan led them to the lounge and invited Jane to sit down on the couch. He sat down on one of the two armchairs and forced a closed smile.

Ethan pointed at the blood-filled syringe that was on the coffee table. "I hope its contents give us everything we need to find out what happened to Christopher."

"Well done. You did a great job. I can only imagine how hard it must have been for you to go to the morgue and get the sample. If you'll excuse me for a minute, I'm going to call a trusted courier company to make arrangements for it to be collected from here and taken to the laboratory that the Apparition Intervention team use."

Ethan waved a hand in the air. "Please, do whatever you need to do so we can uncover the mystery of what had happened to Christopher."

Once she'd made the call, Jane reached into her handbag, took out the A4 photo of Desmond's waistband and handed it to Ethan. "If this photo is anything to go by, then I think the blood sample will give us everything we need, Ethan."

Ethan studied the photo and shook his head. "Jesus Christ. Christopher was doped all right. I'm pretty sure of that looking at the photo. What a devious and conniving way of going about it. It kinda suggests that Desmond was responsible for doping Christopher, but knowing how corrupt illegal cage fighting is, and what goes on behind the scenes, he may not have known anything about it."

"Maybe he did, maybe he didn't, but we can't jump to conclusions just yet. Once I've got the results of the blood tests, I'll be a bit clearer about what I'll do next, but my current thinking is if the tests prove that Christopher was doped then I need to interview Desmond, Dan and the referee. They're the most obvious suspects and the only ones who had contact with Christopher before and during the fight, so I want to start with them and see where that leads me."

Ethan held his hands out to his side and sighed. "You're the investigator so I'll leave that up to you. All I will say is, be careful when you question them. Illegal cage fighting is a big business and controlled in a mafia-like style, so if you go asking the wrong questions to the wrong people, they won't hesitate to . . . how can I put this? Dispose of you, I suppose. My other question is, how are you going to question them without letting them know who you are and who you work for? I don't want any of them to find out that I've hired a private investigator to look into Christopher's death. If they find out it'd be like signing my own death warrant."

Jane cocked her head and raised her eyebrows. "Yes. I can well imagine. Okay, well as I said before, you could introduce me as one of Christopher's aunts and then I can ask some innocent but revealing questions. You should invite all three suspects to the funeral, along with the other guests, and at the wake, you can introduce me to them. That's if they accept the invitation. If they don't, then that might be a clear indication they're too scared or feeling too guilty to go. Obviously, I'll do my best not to ruffle anyone's feathers and pretend that I'm just a concerned and distressed relative who wants to understand what happened to her dear beloved nephew. I can play act when I need to, but there are questions that have to be asked if we're going to find out who was responsible for

Christopher's death."

"Okay. Now I see where you're coming from and I like the idea. That covers us both, and it'll hopefully keep us out of harm's way."

"Good. You'll need to arrange a burial. If anybody asks why he's not being cremated, tell them it was his wishes to be buried."

"Well, that wouldn't be a lie. I spoke to Christopher's mother, Sylvia, earlier and once she'd got over her shock and finished cursing Christopher for not listening to either of us to give up illegal fighting, she confirmed her parents have a burial plot at West Norwood Cemetery and insisted that Christopher be buried there alongside his grandparents."

"Okay. That's great, but you'll have to forewarn Sylvia that Christopher's body may have to be recovered after the funeral so that more tests can be carried out on him if the blood sample doesn't give us any clues, or if it does, but the evidence won't stand up in court. Reassure her that if any further tests have to be carried out, Christopher will be laid to rest beside his grandparents afterward."

"Okay, I'm seeing her tonight for dinner, so I'll talk to her about it. If she thinks it'll help us find Christopher's killer or killers, then I can't imagine she'll object."

"If you think she can be trusted not to tell anybody else, then that's fine."

"I'm sure she'll cooperate if it will help us get to the bottom of what really happened to Christopher and why. Okay. So what day shall we arrange the funeral?"

"I'd say tomorrow, but that might be a bit too quick, and we don't want to arouse any suspicions. What about the day after tomorrow? Do you think that would be all right?"

"I think it would suit Dan fine. As for the others, I have no idea. But as you said, it'll be interesting to know if they accept the invitation. If they don't, it'll be interesting to listen to the excuses they feed me as to why they can't attend."

"Exactly. You could get the ball rolling this afternoon by phoning Dan to let him know and get the telephone numbers for Desmond and Mike if you don't already have them."

"I don't have them actually, but I'm sure Dan will be able to get them for me."

"Perfect. So that's sorted then. Tomorrow I'll go into the office and run some background checks on all three of them to find out if they've got a chequered past which might indicate they're guilty or at least involved in some way or another."

"Okay. I'll call Dan as soon as you've left."

"Excellent. Before I go, it'd be useful if you could give me some background information about Christopher so I can convincingly come across as his close aunt at the funeral and wake. You know . . . his silly quirks and faults. What he liked, what he didn't like. How long you two were together, memorable moments, things he might have told me during phone conversations or when we met in person. His childhood memories. That kinda stuff."

"Yeah, sure. Forgive me if I get a bit upset while I'm doing it, but I'll do my best not to, and give you enough information to make you sound knowledgeable and convincing."

Ethan opened his mouth to speak, and the doorbell rang. Jane looked at Ethan. "That'll probably be the courier. Do you want me to answer the door?"

"Well, I'm not expecting anybody else, so I guess it must be the courier. It's probably best you open the door and greet them. I'm sure my eyes are still a bit red and puffy, so it'll save me some embarrassment."

"Sure. No problem." Jane picked her bag up and took out a small rectangular box. She took the lid off it and leaned forward to pick up the syringe that had Christopher's blood sample in it. She carefully placed it on top of the foam padding and put the padded lid back on. She left the lounge and walked toward the front door.

When she opened it, she was confronted with one of the couriers she knew. "Hi, Mike. Thanks for getting here so quickly. I'm sure I don't need to tell you where it has to be taken?"

"No. Not at all, Jane. The usual place, I guess? I'll get it there as fast as I can and safely."

"That's great, Mike. If you'll excuse me, I'm in the middle of something, so I must go."

"No problem. Me, too. Nice to see you again."

"Likewise. Bye, Mike."

Jane closed the door, walked back to the lounge and sat down. "We should have some news back from the lab by the end of the day."

"That's great. Would you like a drink before I tell you about Christopher and the things you want to know?"

Jane waved a hand. "I'm fine, thanks."

"Okay, but if you don't mind, I'm going to prepare myself one before I start my emotional trip down memory lane."

Jane nodded and smiled. "That's fine. Go ahead. I can imagine you need one after today."

While Ethan was in the kitchen preparing his drink, his head spun thinking of his memories of Christopher. He grimaced and bit his bottom lip knowing he was going to get very emotional recounting all his cherished memories out loud—hearing his own words about their wonderful, loving and unforgettable past together would make it seem all the more real that Christopher was dead and he had a long and painful uphill struggle ahead of him.

Ethan walked back into the lounge and sat down in the armchair where he'd been sitting. He took a sip of his drink and put it on the small table beside him. He looked at Jane, clenched his teeth and shrugged his shoulders. "So where do you want me to start?"

"Well, you could start off by telling me how you and Christopher met."

"Okay. It was actually very romantic because it was a warm sunny day so I went to South Norwood Country Park. It's only a few miles from here, and there's a stunning lake, so I thought it'd be a nice place to chill, sunbathe and take in the sights. I was working from home, as I still do, so it was nice to get out of the house for a while. Given it was such a nice day, a lot of other people had the same idea as me, so space was a bit limited by the lake, but there was a space next to me. I was sitting upright playing patience when out of the corner of my eye I saw Christopher walking toward me. I tried to be as discrete as possible, but I couldn't help turning my head to get a quick glimpse of him. He was wearing a white vest top and a pair of blue nylon shorts which really showed off his impressive muscular frame. I raised my head slightly to acknowledge him, and much to my surprise, he stood close to me and asked if I was expecting any company. When I said I wasn't, he took a towel out of his rucksack and laid it on the grass."

"Aww, that's so sweet. So how old were you when you met him?"

"I was twenty and Christopher was twenty-three."

"So, what happened next? How did you get talking?"

Ethan chuckled and smiled. "Oh, my goodness, I remember it like it was yesterday. After about fifteen minutes, Christopher looked at me and asked me if I fancied a game of cards. I smiled and said it would beat playing cards on my own, so he moved his towel closer to mine. We started off playing pontoon, or twenty-one as some people call it, and we shared some banter because I kept winning. That kinda helped break the ice, and we started to talk about ourselves a bit more. That's when Christopher showed me that he had a very sharp and witty sense of humour. There was a lot of eye contact between us, smiling and laughing, but the thing that kind of gave me the idea he might have liked me was when he asked me to put some sun cream on his back because he felt as if he was getting burned. He explained that because of his physique, he struggled to make sure the whole of his back was covered properly. I timidly said that I would, and my heart was racing as I applied the cream to his herculean back and felt his hard, bulging muscles. Once I'd sat down on my towel, Christopher leaned back and supported himself with his arms. He raised his knees and opened his legs slightly. Without wanting to embarrass you, he didn't have any underwear on, and his shorts were very short, so most of his crown jewels were on display."

Jane laughed out loud and smiled at Ethan. "Oh, you don't have to worry about embarrassing me. I work with three gay guys, and I have a lot of gay friends, and they tell me stories that make my toes curl at times, so that's pretty tame in comparison."

"Well, that's good to hear. So anyway, that was when I was almost certain Christopher was interested in me, and he later told me that he did it deliberately, so I knew what he had to offer . . . and how shall I put this? I was not the least bit disappointed. More impressed if I'm honest. Anyway, when it started to get a bit cool, Christopher suggested we go for a drink, and I agreed. After a couple of drinks, he suggested we go back to his place, which is this place, so we could have dinner together. During dinner, we chatted, and after dinner, we came into the lounge, and he put some music on. When *You Give Me Something* by James Morrison started playing, he took hold of my hand, and I stood up. Then we had a slow dance together, which was so romantic. After that . . . well, he took me to the bedroom, and we made love. And when I say made love, I mean it. It didn't feel like a casual sexual encounter because Christopher was so gentle, passionate and sensual. I remember after we'd made love, we lay in bed staring into each other's eyes and he told me I was the most beautiful man he'd ever met. I felt like putty in his hands and sensed we'd already made a special connection. It was only the following morning while we were eating breakfast, he confessed to me that I'd been the first man he'd ever been to bed with and that all his previous relationships had been with women. He told me he'd always wanted to be with a man, but because of his tough fighting image, he'd been too scared to come out of the closet."

"Oh, wow. That's such a cute and touching story. So how old are you now?"

"I'm twenty-eight now, so Christopher and I had been together for just over eight years. I had hoped we'd grow old and grey together, but that clearly wasn't meant to be."

Jane winced and forced a closed smile. "So what was Christopher like as a person?"

"He was actually quite reserved believe it or not. He may have looked butch and mean, but he was a gentle giant to some extent. That was until someone upset me or him, then the Raging Reynolds side of him came out. He was really focused on his fighting and trained exceptionally hard, normally six days a week. As well as the illegal cage fighting, he also competed in legalised cage fights, so he earned enough to support himself. Given I have my own graphic design company, we were able to live a fairly comfortable lifestyle. We were also saving money for a deposit to buy this place, but I think I'll move and downsize now. This place is too big for me on my own, and to be honest, it holds too many memories of Christopher. I think it's going to be hard enough to get over his death, and I don't think I want to be reminded of it every day."

"That's understandable. So why did Christopher decide to take up cage fighting?"

"Hmm. That's an interesting one but easily answered. When he was younger, he suffered with weight issues, and he got bullied a lot. When his mother, Sylvia, found out, she insisted on him having boxing and karate classes so he could learn to defend himself. I know fighting violence with violence isn't always the answer, but Sylvia decided at the time it was the best thing for her son."

"Oh, that's so sad to hear. I think kids these days can be so cruel to each other, and I think it's got worse now they have access to the internet and can cyber bully."

"That's so true. Anyway, Christopher took to it really well, and once he'd shown the other kids that he could defend himself and get the better of them, the bullying stopped. His passion for karate and boxing didn't stop when he left school though, and he set his sights on becoming a professional fighter. Then when cage fighting became all the rage, it was the natural thing for him to do because it combines all sorts of fighting techniques."

"Okay. You said he was quite a timid and peaceful character outside of the cage. I'm assuming the memories of his childhood days had never left him, and that was what gave him the aggression and fighting spirit he had when he was in the cage."

"You've hit the nail on the head. That and the fact that when he met me, he was initially ridiculed for being gay and he had a point to prove—that a gay man could fight as well as any heterosexual man."

"Yeah, I can imagine. So effectively, the bullying never really stopped, and that drove him."

"Exactly."

"So did you meet any of Christopher's ex-girlfriends?"

Ethan huffed and shook his head. "No, he'd been with a girl shortly before he met me. Marlene, if I remember rightly. From what Christopher told me, she was a spoilt and evil bitch. I thank my lucky stars I've never had the misfortune of meeting her because she sounds like one vicious and nasty piece of work. When they separated, Christopher didn't want anything to do with her, and he certainly wouldn't have wanted to meet up with her or introduce me to her."

"In what way was she a nasty piece of work?"

"She and Christopher met on the cage fighting scene because she was, or still is, a cage fighter. Why she ever took that up, I'll never know. She has a very wealthy father, so she didn't need to do it for the money. I don't know much about her father, but Christopher told me he had his own successful business, but given he came across as being a bit of a gangster, he was almost convinced he was using his business as a front for what he really did to get all the millions he's got. I remember Christopher telling me that when he and Marlene got into an argument, Marlene would literally try to beat him up. The best he could do was defend himself because he refused to hit her."

"Ouch, she *does* sound like a nasty piece of work. I'm not being funny, but I used to be the karate champion for my county, but I've never once dreamt of attacking or hurting my husband when we've had an argument."

Ethan chuckled. "Well, you kept that one quiet. Karate champion of your county, eh. That sounds impressive."

Jane laughed and waved a hand in the air. "Yep, but that was quite some time ago. I still train, though. It kinda comes in handy at times doing the type of job that I do."

"I'm sure it does, and I'm guessing that's why you've been allocated the case?"

"Yep. The owner, Robert, thought I'd be the investigator who'd be able to add the most value. Anyway, final question.

I think I'll skirt around any questions about Christopher's fighting history by saying that I never wanted to talk to him about it. I guess I'll also have to pretend I'm widowed or separated if I'm going to be at the funeral on my own. So, the only other thing I'd like to know is what kind of things Christopher would have talked to me about in person or on the phone?"

"Given what you've just said, he would have constantly been asking you how you are, how you're coping, have you met anybody else, etcetera. Christopher was a very caring person, especially when it came to his family and me."

"Anything else?"

Ethan scratched his head and looked up to his left. "Yeah, I guess there would have been other things when he met you in person. If we'd been on holiday or were planning a holiday, he'd have told you about that. Probably the best thing we can do so you get a real idea of what he would talk to you about is meeting up with his real aunt and his mother before the funeral so you can have a good chat with them."

"That sounds like a great idea. Depending on the time of the funeral we could meet an hour or so beforehand, or tomorrow afternoon. Do his mother and aunt live very far from here?"

"No. They both live within a ten-mile radius, so it shouldn't be too difficult to arrange for us all to meet up beforehand."

"That would be perfect. So where have you and Christopher been on holiday?"

"Okay, I don't think I could handle watching them now, but I have some holiday videos we could watch. I think that'll give you a much better idea of who Christopher was and I can explain where we were. If you want to come back tomorrow afternoon, we can have a look at them and then perhaps go and see Sylvia and his aunt, Patricia, afterwards?"

"That'd be perfect. If you let me know what time Sylvia

and Patricia can meet us, I'll get here an hour earlier."

"That's fine."

"Okay, well, I think I've got as much as I need for the time being, and you're beginning to look a bit worn out so I'll make a move."

"How very observant of you. It's been a busy, trying and emotional day."

Jane stood up, reached out her hand to shake Ethan's. "I understand. Goodbye, and I'll see you tomorrow." Before she left the lounge, she turned back and looked at Ethan. "Please don't forget to send me the names of Dan, Desmond and Mike and call me once you've spoken to them about the funeral."

"Of course I will."

Jane continued to walk and left the lounge. Ethan went to the kitchen and poured himself another drink. He went back into the lounge and placed it on the side table. He reached for his laptop and scrolled through the albums he had in his *iTunes*. The sound of *Over and Over Again,* by Nathan Sykes, filled Ethan's ears, and it was painfully beautiful because it reminded Ethan of Christopher so much. He closed his eyes and filled his mind with wonderful thoughts about Christopher to provide a welcome distraction from the torturous day he'd had.

CHAPTER SEVEN

As Jane drove home, her mind sprang into action. If Ethan was going to tell Christopher's mother what their plan was, her best tactic would be to brief Sylvia on what questions she should ask Dan, Desmond, and Mike. She imagined that if the questions came from Sylvia, none of them would find them out of the ordinary or interrogating. Jane decided that when she spoke to Ethan later that day, she'd put the idea to him to determine if he thought Sylvia would be willing to act as her front at the funeral and wake.

Content that she had a plan in place that would ruffle the least amount of feathers possible, Jane reflected on how moving and endearing it had been to listen to Ethan talking about Christopher so affectionately and lovingly. She was pretty confident that if she had to play act at the funeral and wake, she wouldn't struggle too much.

When Jane approached her local area, she went into auto-pilot. She knew where she was going and started to think about what she could make for dinner for her and her husband, Ricky. Due to the long and quite often unsociable hours she worked, Ricky normally cooked dinner, but because she knew she was going to arrive home early, she thought it'd be a nice treat for him for her to make something special for them. She didn't need to think very hard to know what she was going to prepare—rib eye steak with homemade onion rings—one of Ricky's favourite meals.

Jane stopped at a local supermarket she knew had a decent meat counter to buy what she needed. When she got back to the car, she sent Ricky a message to let him know she was making dinner that night. He quickly responded with emoji's of a smiley face and a love heart. Jane smiled and put the car into gear.

Once she'd parked her car on the driveway, Jane turned the engine off, grabbed her handbag and the bag of groceries on the passenger seat, got out of the car and locked it. She looked at her watch, and it was only 4:50. She grimaced and wondered how long it would take for the lab to call her to let her know what the results of the blood tests were. She was anxious to find out, so she had more clues to go on because she didn't have much else to go on and her theory and potential suspects depended on those results. If Christopher hadn't been doped, she was at a loss as to what avenue she'd pursue next.

When she was inside, Jane went to the kitchen and put the bag of groceries on one of the counters. Before she did anything else, she wanted to get out of her work clothes, which was normally a smart trouser suit and blouse. She wasn't fond of wearing skirts, and they were a nightmare if she had to run after anybody or protect herself in the line of duty.

Feeling more relaxed and comfortable in her casual clothes, Jane went to the stereo and put a Charlie Puth CD on. Then she went to the kitchen and took the groceries out of the bag. She put the rib eye steak on a plate so it would be at room temperature before she cooked it, then set about peeling and cutting the onions before she put them in iced water.

As Jane was in the middle of making the batter for the onion rings, her mobile phone rang. Jane's heart raced in anticipation of it being somebody from the lab calling her. She quickly rinsed her hands under the tap, dried them and reached for her phone. She saw it was the call she'd been waiting for. She quickly accepted the call.

"Hi, Jane, it's Norman here."

"Hi, Norman. Have you got some interesting news for me?"

"I certainly do."

"Go ahead. I'm all ears."

"Well, quite simply put, the deceased died from an overdose of heroin."

Jane gasped and nodded. "That's great news, Norman, and more or less the news I was expecting. Could you be a darling and send me the lab report, so I've got it in writing?"

"I've already sent it to you by e-mail, but I knew you were keen to find out as soon as possible so I thought I'd call you to let you know that it should already be with you."

"You're a star, Norman. Thanks ever so much."

"My pleasure, Jane. Anything else I can do for you?

"Nope. That's all I need to know for the time being."

"In that case, I'll get off the phone and go home. It's been a very long day."

"Sure. Enjoy your evening."

Jane disconnected the call. Feeling relieved the apparition and her gut instincts had been right, Jane decided it was time to treat herself to a small glass of wine. It was early for her to start drinking, but she felt as though she had something to celebrate.

The wine and background music had a soothing effect, and Jane started to unwind, but quickly reminded herself that she still had to call Ethan before she could sign off duty for the day and have a relaxing and romantic night with Ricky.

Jane reached for her phone and scrolled through her contact list until she found Ethan. She suspected he was going to be pleased to hear that Christopher had been drugged, but it wouldn't have surprised her if it angered and confused him to find out that somebody had planned Christopher's death.

Jane hit the call button, and the phone started ringing. After a few rings, the call connected. "Hi, Ethan, it's—"

"Hi, Jane. Have you got any news for me?"

"I certainly do, and the blood tests confirm that Christopher died of a heroin overdose."

"Jesus. So you suspect the needles in Desmond's shorts were connected to vials of heroin?"

"That looks like the most likely way it was injected into him."

"Okay. Am I okay to tell Sylvia? I think she needs to know."

"That's fine. So long as she doesn't accuse Desmond or any of the other suspects of being responsible when we're at the funeral and wake. Until I've done some more digging and got more facts, I don't want anybody but us three to know what we know."

"Yeah. That's fine. I'll tell her, but make her promise not to ruffle anybody's feathers when we meet the suspects in person."

"That's great. As we said before, Desmond may not know anything about it if he's been set up so we can't jump to conclusions at this early stage. One way or another I'll get to the bottom of who's responsible for Christopher's death, but hopefully the background checks I'm going to do tomorrow and meeting the suspects in person will lead me closer to who it is."

"Okay. I'll give you a call tomorrow morning to let you know where and when the funeral's going to take place and brief you on anything else that might be of interest to you."

"That's great. Just before you go, have you spoken to Dan?"

"I have, and he's happy with the proposed date of the funeral, and he's sent me the telephone numbers for Desmond and Mike so I'll give them a call when I get off the phone to you. I'm just waiting for Sylvia to call me to confirm when the service will be held. Hopefully, it'll be the day after tomorrow, but I suppose it all depends on when they can fit us in."

"Okay. Well, let me know once you know. Talking of Desmond and Mike, can you send me a text with their full names? I'll need their details to run the background checks."

"That won't be a problem. Leave it with me, and I'll send you a text as soon as I can."

"Okay. I'll speak to you later or tomorrow, then."

"Okay. Bye."

Jane hung up and reached for her glass of wine. She sat back in her chair, took a sip and let the sound of Charlie Puth fill her ears while she considered if there was anything else that she could do to get to the bottom of Christopher's death. Nothing obvious struck her, so she turned her thoughts to getting everything prepared for dinner.

Ricky arrived back from work at seven. While he went to have a shower and change into his casual clothes, Jane prepared the table and then started cooking.

CHAPTER EIGHT

No sooner had Ethan ended the call with Jane, than his phone rang again. He looked at the screen and saw it was a call from Sylvia. Quickly he swiped the accept call icon and cleared his throat.

"Hi, Sylvia. How are you doing?"

"Not so great, darling, but I wanted to let you know that I've spoken to the people at the cemetery and they can do the burial the day after tomorrow at four in the afternoon. Initially, they said they were fully booked, but after some gentle persuasion, they said they'd work something out so they could accommodate us. I think they normally close at four, so it looks like they're going to stay on a bit later than usual, which I thought was very nice of them."

"Okay, that's great news, because Jane and I had hoped we'd be able to hold the funeral that day so that Jane can meet the suspects as soon as possible. I'll call the undertaker when I get off the phone to you. I was just about to call you actually because we've got the results of the blood tests back, and they've proved that Christopher died of a heroin overdose."

Ethan heard Sylvia gasp. After a momentary pause, she spoke. "So his death was premeditated?"

"It looks like it."

"Okay, we can talk about this more when you get here but I'm telling you now—and forgive me for swearing because I don't normally swear—but I want the bastard or bastards who are responsible for Christopher's death to be found and ideally taken out to sea wearing concrete blocks for shoes. I don't care what has to be done or how much it costs. I want them found and justice to be served . . . legally, or by other means, if you get my drift?"

"I understand perfectly, and I feel exactly the same way."

"Good, so I'll see you about six, and we'll talk some more."

"Sure. I'll get ready and be at yours for six."

"Okay, darling. See you then."

Ethan ended the call and took the undertakers card out of his satchel and called him to let him know what day and time the service was going to be held. He assured Ethan that he would let him know as soon as possible if the horse-drawn carriage was available.

He sent Jane a text message with the full names of Dan, Desmond and Mike and confirmed the funeral would be held the day after next at four. Jane quickly responded, thanking him and that she'd speak to him tomorrow.

As he was drying himself off after his shower, Ethan's stomach started rumbling, and it was then he realised he hadn't eaten anything all day. He was thankful he was going to Sylvia's for dinner because despite feeling hungry, he doubted if he'd have made himself anything to eat if he was at home on his own.

When Ethan arrived at Sylvia's house, he pressed the buzzer by the side of the security gate. Within seconds Sylvia released the lock from inside the house. When he passed through the gate, he shut it and started to walk along the pathway which had grassed lawns either side that were bordered with colourful and perfumed flower beds.

As he approached the front door, Sylvia opened it, stood at the entrance and held her arms out to her side. "It's lovely to see you, Ethan. It feels very strange not seeing you with Christopher, but I'll do my best not to cave in immediately."

Ethan smiled, and as he approached Sylvia, he opened up his arms and embraced her. "It's really strange for me to come here without Christopher, but I guess we'll both have to get used to it, unfortunately."

"I know, darling, but it's hard for both of us. Anyway, come in, so we both don't start crying on the doorstep. That might set the nosy neighbours tongues wagging, and I refuse to give them the satisfaction."

"I'm glad to see you haven't lost your old spirit, Sylvia."

Sylvia stopped, turned to Ethan and chuckled. "Oh, don't get me wrong. Some of them are okay, and I get along with them quite well. But there are others, well . . . they definitely suffer from twitching curtain syndrome. I wouldn't mind, but we don't even have a neighbourhood watch scheme here."

Ethan laughed, put an arm around Sylvia's shoulder, and they continued to walk through the reception area. "You do make me laugh at times, Sylvia. And by the way, you look stunning tonight."

"Why, thank you, my dear. My son may have been murdered, but that's no excuse for letting my appearance go. If you'd have seen me before I put my make-up on and did my hair, I don't think you'd have been so complimentary. I had red blotchy eyes and my hair, well . . . the less you know about how it looked, the better." Sylvia chuckled and put an arm around Ethan's waist. "Come on, let's go into the sitting room, have a little aperitif and get the formalities over and done with before we go through to dinner. I'm afraid dinner is going to be quite simple because I wasn't really in my normal cooking spirit. I'm sure you'll understand and forgive me."

Ethan squeezed Sylvia's shoulder gently and chuckled. "I'm amazed you've been able to prepare anything today, because I haven't eaten a thing, so you could probably put dog food on the table, and I'd probably eat it."

Sylvia laughed out loud and squeezed Ethan's waist. "Withhold your judgement until you've tried it, young man. The last time I looked at the beef bourguignon, it did rather look like that wet dog food that comes in pouches they advertise on TV."

Ethan laughed. "Oh, come on. You're a great cook when you put your mind to it, so I'm sure it'll be lovely."

When they reached the doorway to the sitting room, Ethan removed his arm from around Sylvia's shoulder, and she released her arm from around Ethan's waist. Sylvia led the way into the sitting room, and there was a crystal decanter and two matching glasses on a tray in the middle of the coffee table that was surrounded by two sofas opposite each other.

"I thought we'd have a little sherry to help us relax a bit. Is that okay with you?"

"Yes, that's fine, but I'd better only have the one if I'm going to drive home later."

"Oh, nonsense, Ethan. I'd like you to spend the night here. Being completely selfish, I don't cherish the thought of being in this big house on my own tonight, even though I've been doing it for the past nine years."

"If that's what you'd like, Sylvia, then I'll spend the night here."

"Oh, goody. I feel so much better knowing you'll be here and I'll have company for the evening. Otherwise, I think I'd go out of my tiny mind, constantly thinking about my poor Christopher."

"That's settled then. I'll have a large sherry in that case. I need it after today."

Sylvia poured them both a glass of sherry and handed one to Ethan. "Okay, so shall we make a start? Shall we get the funeral arrangements out of the way first and then you can update me on what's going on with the private investigator."

"Sure, that's fine. Firstly, let me give you the death

certificate. I'm sure it's as fake as the undertaker and the pathologist's report, but you'll need it to register the death." Ethan took the envelope with the death certificate out of his satchel and placed it on the coffee table.

"Thank you, darling. I've already spoken to Penelope who plays bridge with us at the club. She's high up in the registry office and has assured me that she'll fast-track it for me so I can give it to the people at the cemetery before the funeral."

"Aww, that's great and another thing less to worry about. I guess being an upper-middle-class lady who has lots of contacts in high places has its benefits?"

"That it does, my darling. I don't normally like to ask for favours, but this is an exception to the rule."

"Okay, so I wanted to confirm with you that you're happy for the funeral procession to leave from here? It just made more sense to me, given you're closer to the cemetery."

"Oh, absolutely. I insist. I'll speak to my catering company tomorrow to make arrangements for a nice varied buffet, and they can also sort out the drinks and servers."

"Excellent. Now, how many people do you want to invite to the service?"

"Well, given our family seems to be dwindling rather rapidly, it'll be just me and Patricia. Her husband, Charles, is away on business in the middle-east and both her children are working in China, so I suspect they won't be able to make it back in time given the funeral is the day after tomorrow. I'll give Patricia a call tomorrow though just to confirm."

"That's fine. It's just so I know how many cars to order."

"And who are you planning to invite?"

"Well, I know it's going to be really difficult for you, but I need to invite Jane, the private investigator, and the three suspects, Dan, Desmond, and Mike for starters."

Sylvia huffed and took a sip of her sherry. "My goodness. It's going to be so hard to even acknowledge the three suspects, let alone look them in the face or talk to them."

"I appreciate that, and I feel very much the same way, but if we're going to get to the bottom of this, they need to be there. Jane wants to suss them out and gauge their reactions. I'm sure as an investigator . . . she'll see and pick up on things we won't."

"Okay, I'll agree to them coming this time, but once we know who killed Christopher, I want just family and close friends to have a very private and more personal service for him."

"Condition accepted."

"Good. So who else do you want to invite?"

"Only four friends that Christopher and I have been close with since we met. I'm sure you'll remember Tanya and John and Richard and George? You've met them all a few times at our place when we've had dinner parties and barbecues."

"Of course I do. They're all absolute darlings, and I'm sure Christopher would have wanted them to be there. What about Christopher's old friends from school and university?"

Ethan winced and gently shook his head. "Hmm. Unfortunately, when Christopher and I got together, they didn't exactly approve of our relationship, and slowly but surely they fizzled out of his life."

"Ha! What idiots. How petty and ridiculous. Okay. So I've calculated that makes eleven of us. If I'm frank, I don't want any of the suspects in the car with me so you'll have to put them in the second limousine with the other four."

"I completely understand. The seven of them should be able to squeeze into the second car so that shouldn't be a problem. Given Jane is going to pretend she's one of Christopher's aunts, I thought it'd be appropriate for her to come with us in the lead car. Are you okay with that?"

"If there's room for her, then I don't have an issue with it. It'd be nice to get to know her given she's investigating

Christopher's death."

"Well, that brings me nicely onto my next question. Jane would like to meet you and Patricia tomorrow afternoon so she can get to know you both and get a real feel for what Christopher was like as a son and a nephew. She feels it will help her come across more convincingly when she meets the three suspects."

"I think that's a splendid idea. Leave it with me, and I'll mention it to Patricia when I call her tomorrow morning. I'm sure she'll cancel any other plans she's made when I tell her why we need to see her."

"Looks like you're going to be quite busy tomorrow with all the arrangements you need to make."

Sylvia chuckled. "In truth, it's probably best I'm kept busy. Otherwise, I'll just sit around here moping and drowning in my own self-pity."

"Yes, I know the feeling all too well. Okay, so I know I told you we've confirmed that Christopher was doped, but until we see what happens at the funeral, we don't have any other leads at the moment. Jane is hoping that inviting the three suspects to the funeral will be enlightening and give us some more clues as to who doped Christopher. As Jane explained to me—the investigation process is complex, and we need to be patient until the clues start crawling out of the woodwork."

"Okay, but shouldn't she be looking for the shorts that had the needles in them? I'm sure they'd give her lots of clues."

"I appreciate where you're coming from, but I've asked Jane to hold back until after the funeral. I have to tread very carefully here, Sylvia, because if any of the suspects find out that I've gone to the police or hired a private investigator my life would be at risk. You have no idea of the lengths the organisers and bookmakers will go to silence somebody, so we're having to be very careful. Once we've got substantial evidence to convict the person or people who did it, then we can go to the police. But as I said to Jane, if I go to the police now without that evidence, I'd be signing my own death warrant."

"Oh, my goodness, Ethan. I'm so sorry you've got wrapped up in all this. Of course. I completely understand you have to keep everything as hush-hush as possible. Oh, I so hope this Jane knows what she's doing."

"Sylvia. Relax. I knew what I was getting into when I met Christopher, and he knew what risks he was taking. My only concern and focus at the moment is that Jane and I find the person or people who are responsible for Christopher's death. I know it's not going to be easy because our hands are tied in many respects, but I'm sure we'll find them in the end if we're patient and approach things in the right way."

"I pray to God that you do. I'd never be able to live with myself if something happened to you as a direct result of Christopher's choices to fight in illegal fights."

"Don't worry about me. Jane's lovely and she's also the ex-karate champion of her county, and still trains, so she's got some experience and knowledge of how the fighting scene works. Even though I haven't seen her fight, I can well imagine that she'd be more than capable of looking after me and herself. The other thing I don't think I've told you is, Jane has the ability to see apparitions. An apparition appeared in the video I took of the fight, and he paid Jane a visit while she was watching the video. With any luck, he'll reappear and guide us toward the culprit or culprits."

"Okay, well, that's a very strange talent she has, but it's very reassuring to know she's getting some supernatural support. Right, is there anything else we need to talk about before we go through to dinner?"

Ethan shook his head and held his hands out to his side. "Nope. Come on, let's go through for dinner and talk about something else to lift our spirits. So what are you serving the beef bourguignon with?"

"Only boiled rice I'm afraid, my dear. But I have a fabulous bottle of wine that might compensate for what might turn out to be a disastrous meal."

"That sounds good to me. Come on, let's get started."

As they walked along the corridor to the kitchen, Sylvia turned back and looked at Ethan. "I've set the table in the kitchen given it's just me and you, but if you'd rather, I can set the table in the dining room. I just thought it'd be a bit formal in the dining room. At least in the kitchen, it'll be a bit more casual and intimate."

"Oh, the kitchen's fine with me. I think with just you and me in the dining room, it would seem a bit empty."

"Exactly. Not that we would, but could you imagine, you and I sat at opposite ends of a table that seats twelve people? It would seem very strange, albeit somewhat regal."

As they entered the kitchen, Ethan looked to the right and saw that Sylvia had made an effort to make the table look inviting and welcoming. "There was really no need to go to so much trouble, Sylvia."

"Trust me, I haven't gone to that much trouble, darling. I've only put a table cloth on the table and a few candles. Right, you go and sit yourself down, and I'll be back in a jiffy with dinner. The wine's decanted so help yourself. Just make sure you pour me a glass, but you don't have to wait for me to start on yours."

"Thank you, and the table looks very nice." Ethan walked toward the table. The candles gave the dining area a warm and cosy feel, and Ethan recalled the times when he and Christopher had gone there for dinner, and the three of them had eaten at the table together. His only hope was his emotions wouldn't take control when he started eating, prompting him to throw up what he'd chewed and tried to swallow. The lump in his throat had come back again, and he reassured himself that if he just took small mouthfuls and ate slowly, he'd be able to keep the food down.

When he reached the table, he sat down on one of the seats that enabled him to see Sylvia in the kitchen. He carefully picked the wine decanter up and poured a glass of wine for Sylvia before he served himself. He took a sip and hoped the effects of the alcohol would dull his senses and emotions a bit before he tried to eat.

Ethan watched Sylvia as she served the rice on the plates. His heart sank, and he truly felt for her as he noticed her hands shaking, and her head hung low. Once she'd managed to ladle the beef bourguignon on top of the rice without spilling it everywhere, she picked up the plates, turned around and started to walk toward the table. "You know . . . my instinct is to talk about Christopher, but that probably wouldn't do either of us any good at the moment, and I'm sure I'll get my opportunity to talk about him when we meet Jane tomorrow." Sylvia handed one of the plates to Ethan and put the other plate at her place setting.

"Thank you, Sylvia, and if you feel the need to talk about Christopher, then I'm fine with that. But as you said, I'm sure Jane will want to know as much as you can tell her tomorrow so you'll have your opportunity."

"That's very sweet of you, darling, but tonight let's try to focus on something else. In fact, I was thinking that after dinner we could go downstairs to the TV lounge and watch an old film. I'm physically and mentally drained at the moment, so I think a film might provide some welcome distraction."

"That's also fine with me so long as it's *Blade Runner*. That was probably Christopher's all-time favourite film."

"You've got a deal. It's one of my favourite films also, and if I'm not mistaken, I was the one who introduced him to it — it was released a bit before his time — the early eighties if I remember correctly, so he wasn't even born."

"I think you could be right there. He introduced it to me, so somebody must have introduced it to him."

"Yes, I'm pretty sure it was me. Anyway, tell me, what are your plans for the future? Do you plan to stay where you are or move somewhere else?"

"Hmm. Funny enough, I had the same conversation with Jane earlier. My initial thoughts are to move to a smaller place. Not only because paying the rent on that place on my own would be a bit of a struggle, but I think I'd be constantly plagued by the memories I have from living there with Christopher."

"That's understandable, but if you do want to stay there, and it's just money that's stopping you, then you only have to ask."

"That's very kind of you, but I'll see how I feel when the rental contract is due to expire in just over a month."

"So if you do move, where do you think you'll move to? Not far from here, I hope?"

"I haven't really given it much thought yet, but I'll let you know as and when I've done some research on areas, prices, and what I can get for my money."

"Okay, darling, but it goes without saying that you're more than welcome to move in here if you're still not sure where you want to go when your rental agreement's up. It might do us both good to have company until we've had time to come to terms with what's happened to Christopher and deal with it in our own ways."

"That's a very generous offer, and you never know, I might just take you up on that offer if I don't feel confident about confronting the big bad world on my own."

"Excellent. Well, that's settled then. So, what do you think of my *creation*?"

"It's actually really nice, but if I'm honest, I'm eating out of politeness more than desire."

Sylvia chuckled, leaned forward and placed a hand on Ethan's. "I know exactly what you mean. I feel the same way, but we both have to try to eat something. Eat as much as you feel comfortable with and leave what you don't want. Given the circumstances, I won't be the least bit offended." Ethan forced a smile and took another small mouthful.

Once they'd both eaten as much as they could, Sylvia took the plates, went to the kitchen and scraped what was left on them into the bin. Once she'd put them into the dishwasher, she walked toward Ethan. "Come on. Let's go and watch that film, and we'll finish the wine while we're watching it. You grab the wine decanter, and I'll get us some fresh glasses."

"Sure thing. I'll meet you in the TV lounge. I take it the DVD is still in the bottom of the TV cabinet?"

"It certainly is. I'll be with you in a tick. Ooh, this should be fun. I haven't spent a night at the movies with anyone for ages."

"Well, we'll probably both blubber throughout the whole film thinking about Christopher, but maybe that's what we both need to do, and when better to do it than when we're together."

"I'm sure you're right, and I couldn't agree with you more. Go on then. Go to the TV lounge and set it all up. I just want to tidy up here a bit, and then I'll join you."

"Do you want me to help?"

"No. Don't be silly. It'll only take me a few minutes."

Ethan stood up and grabbed the wine decanter. He made his way downstairs to the basement that Sylvia had converted into a TV lounge. He turned the light on and walked toward the coffee table, where he placed the wine decanter on a place-mat in the centre. Ethan was hit with a wave of nostalgia as he recalled the times when they'd all sat and watched films there together.

Determined to be strong for Sylvia's sake, Ethan made

himself busy and went to the TV cabinet. He opened the doors of the bottom unit and searched through the DVD's until he found the case for Blade Runner. He turned the DVD player on and pressed eject, just in case there was still a DVD in it, but nothing came out. He put the DVD in the player, stood up and opened the doors of the top unit to reveal the huge flat screen TV with surround sound that made watching any film feel like you were at the movies.

When Sylvia arrived with the wine glasses, she poured them both a glass of wine before sitting on the sofa next to Ethan. Once they were settled, Ethan used the remote controls to start the film and dim the lights to add to the cinematic effect.

While they were watching the film, the inevitable happened, and they both recounted some of their memories of Christopher and how much they wished he was sat there with them on the sofa. Thankfully the lighting was dim, so when a tear escaped Ethan's eye, he was able to wipe it away discretely so Sylvia didn't notice. Based on her hand movement, he was almost certain Sylvia was having to do the same thing, but in some ways, it did feel as if Christopher was with them—in spirit, even though not in person.

Once the film had finished, they both agreed it was time for them to go to bed. Ethan turned the TV and DVD player off, and they both made their way to the second floor of the house. Even though Sylvia told Ethan he was free to sleep in any of the spare bedrooms, he assured her he wanted to sleep in the room where he and Christopher had always slept when they'd stayed at Sylvia's. It was familiar, and Ethan knew he'd feel that bit closer to Christopher if he slept there.

CHAPTER NINE

When Jane arrived at the Apparition Intervention offices, the smell of cooked bacon from the local café she'd passed still lingered in her nostrils and her mouth watered. She indicated to turn left into the narrow driveway that led to the car park at the rear of the building. As she pulled into the turning, she caught a glimpse of the sign screwed to the wall, which stated *Strictly for the use of Apparition Intervention personnel and their clients.* She chuckled to herself because she'd lost count of the number of times people going to the local shops had parked in her car parking space, even though there was a sign stating it was reserved for her. She'd had to leave notes on windscreens of the owner's cars on several occasions asking them not to park in her space again. Otherwise, she'd call the police.

When she entered the car park, she looked at her space on the left-hand side and breathed a sigh of relief—her stream of notes had started to have the desired effect. As she reached for the ignition key, she glanced at the clock on the dashboard and was pleased to see it was just before nine in the morning. She grabbed her handbag and mobile phone from the hands-free cradle, locked the car and started walking toward the back entrance of the building. As she was about to swipe her entry card, her stomach rumbled, and it reminded her she'd skipped breakfast.

Jane put her swipe card back in her handbag and started walking toward the driveway that led to the main road. She craved a nice bacon sandwich to get her day off to a satisfying and filling start. As she walked along the driveway, Jane called Martine.

"Hi, Jane. Everything okay? How's the new case going?"

"Everything's moving along as well as can be expected. Anyway, I'll tell you about that very soon. I'm outside the office, but I need something to eat so I'm going to get a bacon sandwich. I was calling to find out if you fancied one?"

"Ooh, that'd be very naughty, but why the heck not? It's not like I eat one for breakfast every day, and it'll make a nice change from a boring muesli bar."

"Right. That's sorted then. I'll see you in about five or ten minutes so you'll have plenty of time to get the kettle on and make us both a nice cup of tea."

Martine chuckled. "Why, you cheeky mare. Just kidding. You've got a deal."

"Great. I'll see you soon then. Oh, is Robert in?"

"He's out this morning at meetings, but he'll be here later if you need to speak to him."

"Well, let's see how I get on this morning, and then I'll know if I need to speak to him or not. Right. See you soon. One sugar for me, don't forget."

Martine laughed. "I haven't. How could I? You drink so much tea, it'd be impossible to forget."

"Okay. See you soon." Jane ended the call and continued to walk toward the café, which was about twenty metres from the office. Although the morning air was still quite fresh, the sky was clear blue, and it showed signs of being another glorious Indian summer day.

Once she had the bacon sandwiches, she made her way to the office, and when she walked in, Martine was sitting at her desk expectantly waiting and greeted her with a broad smile and a cheeky glint in her eyes.

Martine pointed at the two cups of tea on her desk and beckoned Jane to sit down in front of her desk. "Right. I've kept to my side of the bargain so come on, hand it over. I'm so looking forward to my naughty treat."

Jane chuckled and handed Martine one of the sandwiches which was wrapped in a white paper bag. "I'd hardly call it a naughty treat, but knowing how you like to stay so slender and toned I guess it is for you."

"Oh, you bet it is. Did you get any sauces?"

"Yep. There's a sachet of red and brown sauce in with your sandwich."

"Fab! It's gotta be the brown with bacon."

As they ate their sandwiches and drank their tea, Jane gave Martine an update on the previous day's events and told her she'd gone to the office to run some background checks on the main suspects. Martine reassured her that if she needed any help, then she'd do whatever she could to assist.

Once they'd finished breakfast, Jane went to her desk and turned her computer on. She was eager to find out if Dan, Desmond or Mike had a chequered past which might indicate they could have been responsible for killing Christopher.

When she was in the records database, Jane typed in Dan's full name in the search bar and waited for the results to come back. His record list was short, with only three entries, but one of the records grabbed her attention—a court case that took place in 1999.

Jane clicked on the link and started reading the court report. Her eyes widened when she saw that the charge had been brought against Dan by Michael James Anderson—the referee, Mike.

During a fight between Dan and Mike's son, Trevor, Dan had knocked Trevor out but continued to unnecessarily punch and kick him, despite the referee doing his best to stop Dan from hurting Trevor any more. The judge convicted Dan to five years' imprisonment for violating cage fighting standards of behaviour, being unethically aggressive, and causing irreparable brain damage to Trevor Anderson. He served his time in Wormwood Scrubs and was released on parole after serving three years of his sentence.

Jane sat back in her chair and breathed out heavily. Her suspicious mind had already taken over. Given Mike knew Dan viewed and treated Christopher as if he was his own son, what better way to get revenge for the damage Dan had caused to his son? She knew she couldn't jump to conclusions, but it certainly gave Mike the motive to kill Christopher, and he certainly had access to all sorts of drugs, so he had the means.

The remaining question was the how? How would he have been able to get access to Desmond's shorts so he could have placed the syringes in his shorts? In some ways that could have implied that Desmond worked in collaboration with Mike. But why would Desmond want to kill Christopher apart from winning the fight? Jane couldn't imagine anyone would go to that extreme to win a fight.

No sooner had she developed a theory, she saw it rapidly crumbling and falling apart as she thought through the finer details of it. Mainly, the how?

Convinced she might be onto something, Jane quickly looked at the other two records under Dan's name. They were both minor incidents of actual bodily harm dating back to when he was a teenager and in his early twenties. He got his wrists slapped, and nothing more came of the incidents.

Jane didn't know whose records to check next—Mike or Desmond? Keen to determine if Desmond had a motive for wanting to kill Christopher, which might have led him to collaborate with Mike, Jane decided to check his records first. She went back to the search bar and typed in Desmond Osborne.

It came as no surprise to Jane that he had a number of minor convictions for actual bodily harm and was caught by the police several times smoking marijuana when he was in his teenage years. When she got to the end of the list of records, Jane thought she may have struck gold—four months prior, Desmond was forced into bankruptcy by a number of his creditors because he owed them in excess of one-hundred-fifty-thousand pounds. Given his business had been on the verge of ruin and he had no other means of repaying his creditors, his house was repossessed to pay off his outstanding debts.

Jane sat back in her chair and stroked her temples with her hand. She struggled to imagine that Desmond would kill Christopher in exchange for a bribe to rig the fight, but if he was financially ruined, he might just have done it if the bribe had been big enough. But who would pay Desmond what she imagined would have to be an extortionate amount of money to rig the fight? Let alone kill Christopher in such a public place and in the manner that he'd been killed. Surely any fool would have realised they'd be a prime suspect and wouldn't get away with it?

The other thought that struck Jane was Dan had told Ethan the cause of death was a severe injury to the head. Why would he have lied to Ethan to mask the truth? Did he have something to hide? The only motive he would have had would have been money, but if he thought so much of Christopher and treated him like a son, then surely no amount of money would be enough to kill him?

Jane's concentration was broken when she felt what she assumed was Martine's hand on her shoulder. She turned around, and Martine was standing behind her.

"I'm going to make myself another cup of tea. Do you want one?"

"Oh, yes please, and it'd be even better if you put a nip of Brandy in it."

Martine clenched her teeth and screwed her face up. "Oh,

dear. That bad is it?"

"You could say that."

"Why? What's wrong?"

"Oh, nothing. I'm just getting more confused by the minute, and nothing is making sense right now."

"Why's that?"

"Well, I've run background checks on two of the prime suspects and while both of them may have had a motive for killing Christopher, I honestly don't believe either of them would have."

"And what would that motive be?"

"Money. Receiving a bribe to fix the fight."

"What? By doping someone with heroin? They'd have to be pretty bloody stupid to have rigged the fight in that way in front of hundreds of people."

"Yep. My thoughts exactly. And that's why I'm getting confused."

"So how many other suspects do you have to look into?"

"Just the one at the moment."

"In that case, I'd suggest you look into that one while I go make us both a nice cup of tea and when you've looked at their records, we can have another chat."

"Yeah. You're right. I'll just have to keep digging until I come up with something a bit more solid."

Martine patted Jane on the back and smiled. "That's the spirit. Never give up hope."

"Yeah, you're right. Okay, go and make that tea, and I'll crack on here."

"Okay, I'll see you in five minutes."

Jane printed out the record of Desmond's bankruptcy and went back to the search bar. She typed in Michael James Anderson and hit the enter button. When the results came back, the title and a brief description of one of the records shone a little brighter than the others which struck her as being odd.

Intuitively she looked to her left and right, but there was no sign of the apparition. She clicked on the record and started to read it.

Jane nodded her head and smirked as she read the account of when Mike had been under police surveillance for drug dealing and was raided one night at three in the morning. The police confiscated an assortment of pills and liquids that later transpired to be illegal pain killers and physical performance enhancers. But in addition to the drugs, they found two-hun-dred-fifty-thousand pounds in cash. When they'd asked him where he got the money from, Mike had claimed it was the winnings from a large bet he'd made. Not convinced he was telling the truth, the police confiscated the money as well as the pills and liquids.

Given the money was all in used notes, couldn't be traced and they couldn't prove the money was from a bribe as opposed to a bet, the police returned the money within a matter of months. Mike was put on probation for a year and banned from selling any type of illegal substances, but that was six years prior, so Jane suspected he was off the police radar and could still be dabbling in the sale of them.

"So how's it going?" Martine asked in a cheerful manner.

"Well, I'm not sure if my apparition friend is helping me, but when I searched for the records of the third suspect, one of the records had a distinct glow to it, and it may offer some clues."

Martine put Jane's cup of tea down on a coaster on her desk and stood beside her. "Ooh. Tell all. That sounds promising."

"Yeah, you might want to take a seat. I'm still trying to make sense of what I've just read."

Martine walked around to the front of Jane's desk and sat down. "Okay, so what have you just read?"

Jane briefly explained what the police report had stated, placed her elbows on her table and held her hands out to the side. "So there you have it. I just find it strange that the record was highlighted, but there was no sign of the apparition. Maybe it's just a fluke and a false lead."

"Hmm. Given the guy has a quarter of a million pounds in cash, I can't imagine money would have been his motivation."

"No, me neither. Unless of course, a quarter of a million pounds isn't enough for him, and he got greedy."

"Hmm. I'm not entirely convinced."

"Nope. Neither am I. The other theory I have is that Mike wanted revenge because Dan, Christopher's coach, treated him like a son, and ironically Dan had a fight with Mike's son and caused him permanent brain damage. Now that could be his motivation—to get even with Dan for destroying his and his son's life."

"Now that one I could believe. But why would he do it in a public place where so many people could witness the death of Christopher? And . . . he doesn't have any previous convictions for heroin, or any other similar type of drug."

"Yeah, that's what I can't get my head around." Jane sighed. "I was hoping that doing some background checks would help me get one step closer to who killed Christopher, but it's just given me more theories and doubts than I had before. My only hope now is that I can get a better impression of the three suspects tomorrow when I meet them at the funeral, and they might unconsciously give some clues away."

"Okay. So the funeral's tomorrow?"

"Yeah. At four o'clock in the afternoon, then I'll go back to the wake. I also want to go and have a look at the warehouse where it all happened. I wanted to go yesterday, but I had a pretty full-on day, so I thought I'd leave it until after the funeral, and I've met the suspects."

"Well, it sounds like you have a game plan, so don't beat yourself up just yet. It's still early days, and you've only been on the case a couple of days. Rome wasn't built in a day, you know!"

"Yep. This is very true. I guess I'll just have to be a bit more patient."

"You do that. Right, I'm going to get back to work, but let me know if I can help in any way."

"Yeah, sure, but I think I've got it under control at the moment."

As Jane sat at her desk, drinking her tea and pondering what to do next, her mobile phone rang. She looked at the screen and saw it was a call from Ethan, so she pressed the accept call button. "Hi, Ethan. I take it . . . you've got some news for me."

Ethan sighed. "Yes, I certainly do. Before I tell you though, we can go and see Sylvia and Patricia at any time after two. What time suits you best?"

"Well, I've done practically everything I can do here, so the sooner, the better."

"Okay, if you get to me about a quarter to two, I'll phone Sylvia when I get off the phone to you to let her know that we'll be there at two."

"If you want, I can get there earlier, and we can watch some of the video footage of you and Christopher?"

Ethan cleared his throat. "Jane, if it's all right with you, I'd rather we watched that when we get back from Sylvia's. I know I'll get choked up and the last thing I want to do is turn up at Sylvia's house with red blotchy eyes. I need to be as strong as I can when I meet Sylvia and Patricia, and I know I'll be a complete emotional wreck if we watch the videos beforehand."

"That's fine. I completely understand. I'll grab a bite to eat here soon and then make my way over to your place."

"Thanks for understanding. Now I'll tell you what may prove to be some interesting news."

"Fire away. I'm all ears."

"Well, I spoke to Dan, and obviously he's going to be at the funeral. Mike seemed a bit hesitant and reluctant, but eventually confirmed he'd attend. Desmond however . . ."

"He's not going?"

"Nope. I spoke to his girlfriend, who's ironically called Marlene, and she told me Desmond was absolutely devastated about Christopher's death because he feels responsible. Marlene told me his doctor has put him on heavy sedatives, and he's in no fit state to leave the house, let alone attend the funeral."

"Okay, well, that's kind of understandable."

"Hang on. I haven't told you the best part yet."

"Oh, right. And what's that?"

"Marlene claims to have known Christopher and said she'd attend the funeral on Desmond's behalf so they can both pay their last respects to him."

"Hmm. That's interesting. Do you think she's the Marlene that Christopher used to date?"

"Ha! You're guess is as good as mine, but it sounds kinda coincidental, don't you think?"

"Very. So did you tell her she was welcome to attend the funeral?"

"I did . . . because half of me is curious to find out if she is the Marlene that Christopher had a relationship with. I'd also like to know what she looks like and what she has to say for herself on behalf of Desmond."

"Yes, you're right. Smart thinking."

Ethan chuckled. "I do my best, and I thought you'd want to meet her."

"I certainly do, because if she is the Marlene that Christopher had a relationship with, then I'd really like to know what she's doing with Desmond and how long she's been with him."

"Yes, the same thought crossed my mind. Another

coincidence, perhaps?"

"Who knows at the moment, but hopefully we'll find out tomorrow."

"Do you know if they ended on bad terms?"

"Christopher and I never really spoke about his relationship with her, but from what I can gather, they certainly didn't end on good terms. Perhaps Sylvia knows a bit more than I do so we can ask her about it later."

"Yeah, sure, that's fine. Listen, before I go. Could you write down the directions to get to the warehouse where the fight took place? I want to go and have a little snoop around at some point, after I've met all of the suspects, to see if I find any clues there."

"That's fine. I'll let you have them when you get here. It's only a twenty-five-minute drive from here, and it's pretty straightforward to get to."

"That's great. Right. I'll let you go, and I'll see you at one-forty-five."

"Okay. See you later."

Jane hung up, stroked her chin with her hand and frowned. With the introduction of Marlene—if it was the Marlene that Christopher had dated—she suspected things were going to get even more interesting and complex. If they'd ended on bad terms and she still held a grudge against Christopher, she might have been responsible for doping Christopher. Jane suspected the last thing she'd have wanted was for her current boyfriend to have the crap kicked out of him and lose the fight to her ex-boyfriend who'd left her to be with a man.

With another potential suspect and theory, Jane wanted to try and find out who the apparition she'd seen was. She hoped if she could track him down and find a bit out about his history, it might give her some more clues.

Jane went to the initial enquiry screen of the database and typed *males between the ages of twenty-five and thirty who have died of a drug overdose in the Upper Norwood area in the past five years.*

When the results came back, her monitor was filled with photos of men's faces with their names and dates of death underneath them. As she looked at the top left-hand corner of her screen, she saw the face of the apparition who'd been called Ricky Richards. There was no mistaking his gaunt face, long pointed nose and hollow looking eyes.

Jane looked at the date underneath the photo and calculated that he'd died five days before Christopher's fight with Desmond which struck her as being very coincidental. She hoped that when she read his records, she'd be able to link him to one of the suspects, so she clicked on the photo and was taken to the notes section.

Jane read with interest that although his name had been Ricky Richards, he was more commonly known as Ricky the Rat because his face was so gaunt and his nose was so long and pointed. He'd also earned the nickname because he'd rat on anybody, even so-called friends, to get his next fix.

Ricky grew up with his mother, two elder brothers and younger sister on a rough council estate in Upper Norwood. His father had left his mother when he was fifteen and when his mother took in a new boyfriend, Ricky had been subjected to frequent beatings, so he left home and slept rough on the streets. That was why Ricky had become involved in drugs, specifically heroin—while living on the streets, he'd come into contact with junkies who got him onto the stuff, and then he got hooked.

Ricky had a string of minor burglary offences which came as no surprise to Jane because most junkies did. He'd beg, steal or borrow to get his next fix and quickly became involved in drug dealing to pay for his own drugs.

He'd been warned and charged by the police several times for drug dealing offences. The first couple of times, he'd had his wrist slapped because the amounts he'd been caught with had been so minimal it wasn't worth charging him. But on the third occasion, he was sentenced to a year in prison. During that time, he cleaned himself up, but as soon as he'd got out, he went back to his old ways.

The police continued just to give him warnings because he was considered to be a lost cause and so far down the drug supply chain that he wasn't important enough for them to waste their limited resources on. They had bigger fish to fry and bigger drug dealers to focus on.

Jane sat back in her chair, cupped her mouth with her hand and blew out rapid spurts of air. What she'd read about Ricky hadn't given her anything to connect him to any of the suspects. As interesting as it was to have found out who he was and when he'd died, it didn't serve any real purpose. The fact that he'd died of a drug overdose five days before the fight intrigued Jane, and she suspected his death could have been linked to one of the suspects, but there was no evidence or association to prove it. Given Ricky was dead, Jane concluded there was a very slim chance of her ever being able to find out.

Feeling frustrated and confused, Jane shut her computer down, said goodbye to Martine and went to a local sandwich shop and ordered a pastrami and dill sandwich on rye bread and a cup of tea to eat in.

CHAPTER TEN

While Jane was driving to Ethan's house, even though her eyes were focused on the road, her mind was focused on the new information she'd found out about the prime suspects. Even though she knew the following day was going to be an awful and emotional day for Ethan, Sylvia, and Patricia, she was looking forward to it so she could meet Dan, Mike, and Marlene. Not having met them in person, all she could base her theories and suspicions on were the video of the fight, what she'd been told by Ethan, and the information the police records had given her.

When she arrived at Ethan's, she knocked on the door, and when he answered, she smiled. "Are you ready to leave?"

"Yeah, just let me grab my satchel and keys, and I'll be back."

"No problem, take your time." Ethan returned, closed and locked the door. Jane looked at him. "Do you want me to drive?"

"That'd be great if you don't mind. I think it's probably best for you to drive, just in case I get upset when we're talking to Sylvia and Patricia."

"Yeah. And if I drive, I'll probably remember how to get to Sylvia's tomorrow."

While Jane drove, Ethan talked her through the directions to get to the warehouse. Jane assured him that, providing she had the directions written down, she'd be able to find it. In the unlikely event she did get lost, she said she'd call him.

"Okay, if you turn left at the end of the road, then we'll be in the road where Sylvia lives," Ethan announced.

As they drove along Sylvia's road, Jane was in awe of how stunning the houses were.

Ethan pointed at a house on the right. "Pull up outside that one."

Jane parked the car and looked at Ethan. "Wow. That is an impressive looking house."

"Yes, it's beautiful, isn't it? Christopher's father was an architect, and he earned good money. Unfortunately, he paid an early price for his success."

"Oh, dear. What happened?"

"He had a massive heart attack about nine years ago and died immediately. There was nothing the paramedics could do when they arrived at his offices, so that was that. It's such a shame because I never got to meet him, but then again, maybe Christopher wouldn't have come out of the closet if he was still alive. Who knows?"

"Oh, my goodness. So Sylvia must be absolutely devastated now that she's lost Christopher?"

"I don't really think the reality of what's happened has really sunk in yet, but it will at some point and I think it's going to hit her really hard."

"Well, I'm sure you'll do what you can to prop her up and help her cope with her tragic loss."

"I'll do whatever I can, but I don't think my grieving has really started yet. I think because both of us know that Christopher was deliberately murdered our focus is on finding out who murdered him. I think when we've got to the bottom of that, and justice has been served, then we'll both be hit hard."

"Well, I hope that we'll find out who killed Christopher very soon, so you can both move on, grieve, and then focus on your futures."

Ethan sighed and blew out air. "In many respects, that's the best thing, but I'm worried about how hard it's going to hit us both when this is all over and done with."

"I don't wish to sound patronising, but you could always consider grievance counselling if things get that bad. I know it really helps a lot of people."

Ethan smiled and nodded his head. "Well, if either one of us gets too bad, then I think that'd be a wise move. Anyway, let's go and meet Sylvia and Patricia. First things first. I'll worry about how we're going to handle the grieving as and when it happens."

"Sure. Come on then, let's go."

When they reached the front gate, Ethan pressed the intercom buzzer. "I'll do my best to put on a brave face, as I'm sure Sylvia and Patricia will, but don't be surprised if one of us, or all three of us, break down at some point. This is going to be very emotional for all of us."

Jane put a hand on Ethan's arm. "You wouldn't be human if the emotions didn't get to you. I think I'm prepared, but I know it's going to be extremely difficult for all of you."

The gate buzzed, and Ethan opened it. He waited for Jane to pass through and then led the way to the front door. Within seconds it opened and a slender, elegant woman wearing a simple black fitted tunic dress, who appeared to be in her mid-fifties, opened it. She smiled at Ethan and put a hand out to shake Jane's. "Hello, Jane, I'm Sylvia, Christopher's mother. Please . . . please come in."

Ethan indicated that Jane should go in first. Jane stepped forward, and Sylvia moved to one side so she could pass her. Once she was in the reception area, she turned around, and as Ethan entered, he and Sylvia kissed each other on both cheeks and briefly hugged.

Sylvia turned to Jane. "Please, follow me. I thought we'd have some tea in the sitting room." Sylvia led the way, and Jane and Ethan followed her. As she walked through the reception area toward the sitting room, she didn't look back. "I wish I could say it's a pleasure to meet you, Jane, but given the circumstances, I'm sure you'll understand that I can't, but please don't let that stop you from feeling comfortable in my home. I fully understand why you're here, and the sooner we can find out who killed my son, the better. I won't settle until the person or people responsible for Christopher's death are found, and justice is served. I'll refrain from telling you how I'd like to see justice served because a prison cell is far too good for whoever did it. An eye for an eye and a tooth for a tooth, and all that."

"I completely understand, Sylvia, and I'm sorry to have to put you and Patricia through this, but I'm sure Ethan has explained my reasons for wanting to see you both."

Sylvia stopped and turned around to look at Jane. "Yes, he has, Jane, and for that reason, you are more than welcome in my house. My only hope is that you're as good as Ethan proclaims you to be."

"Well, I've managed to solve every case I've worked on to date, and I see no reason why this case should be any different."

"Good. That's very reassuring to hear. And I don't care what Ethan says . . . when you've finished your work on the case, as you put it, your company should send the invoice to me."

Ethan interjected. "Come on, Sylvia."

"Nonsense, Ethan. You have enough to worry about at the moment, and the last thing you need to worry about is money. I'm in a far better position to pay the bill, so that's that. I'll hear no more of it."

Jane cleared her throat. "Okay. Well, we can talk about that once I've finished my work. The main priority now is finding out who killed Christopher."

"Good. I like your attitude, Jane. Right, shall we go through to the sitting room? I'll ask Patricia to make us some tea."

Without further hesitation, Sylvia turned around and walked toward the sitting room. As they entered, Jane looked around the vast sitting room, and it was as impressive as the photos she'd seen in homes and gardens magazines. The modern, yet rustic décor gave it a chic and classy look—very much like the owner.

As they approached the sofas, an equally elegant woman dressed in black stood up and reached her hand out to shake Jane's. She looked slightly older than Sylvia, but Jane could see the family resemblance. "Hello, Jane, if you hadn't already worked it out, I'm Patricia, Sylvia's sister. I couldn't help overhearing what Sylvia said when you both arrived, so I won't repeat what she's already said."

"That's perfectly fine, and I completely understand."

Patricia and Ethan greeted each other in the same way Ethan had greeted Sylvia. Sylvia invited Jane and Ethan to sit on one of the sofas, and she sat on the sofa opposite them.

Patricia remained standing and looked at Sylvia. "I'll just go and make some tea, but feel free to make a start without me."

"Thank you, darling."

Patricia left the sitting room, and Sylvia looked at Jane. "So, where do you want to start? I've been through the old videos, so I thought we could go downstairs to the TV lounge once we've had a chat and finished our tea. I thought it might be helpful if you saw some footage of when Christopher was a young boy and how he changed over the years."

"That would be perfect, Sylvia. Okay, so if we're going to watch some videos, I'm sure you can talk me through them and explain how Christopher's transition took place?"

"I certainly can. I think the last video footage I have of him was while he was still living here. I think Ethan can probably show you some videos of their life experiences together."

"Jane and I are going to look at those when we get back to

our place," Ethan replied.

"Okay, well, they say a picture paints a thousand words, so I'm not sure what else I can tell you about Christopher, Jane."

"There is one thing that Ethan and I are curious to know."

"And what's that?"

"Do you remember the girl, Marlene, that Christopher had a relationship with?"

"Oh, that wretched Marlene. I met her once and told Christopher I never wanted to meet her again and that he should dump her. Such a vile, vindictive, possessive and rude young woman. If I'm honest, Christopher was very apprehensive about telling me he was gay, but when he told me he'd met Ethan, I was elated because he seemed so happy. As far as I was concerned, that was the most important thing, and if it meant he'd stay away from that Marlene, then I was even more comfortable with the idea of him having a relationship with another man. And then, of course, when I met Ethan, he won me over with his charm and strikingly good looks."

"You'll have me blushing in a minute, Sylvia," Ethan jested.

"Nonsense. It's true. You both made such a lovely couple, and your love for each other stood the test of time. It's just heart-breaking to know he won't be around anymore for either of us."

"Well, he'll always remain in our hearts, Sylvia, and we'll never forget our memories of him, so he may not be with us in person, but he's here with us in spirit."

Sylvia's face flushed red, and she leaned forward. "That may be so, but I won't rest until whoever took him away from us pays the price for what they've done."

"That may be so, but one thing at a time," Jane interjected. "Would you recognise her if you saw her?"

"Probably. She's got one of those faces that are hard to

forget."

"How would you describe her?"

"I think she tries to base her look on that actress. Oh, what's her name?" Sylvia cupped her forehead with her hand. "Bear with me, it'll come to me in a minute." She looked up to her left and tapped her chin with her hand repeatedly. "That's it! Bridget Neilson. You know . . . the actress that was with Sylvester Stallone."

"Okay. So is she as tall as Bridget Neilson?"

"They're about the same height, yes, but Bridget Neilson is far more attractive. Marlene may think she's got the looks to pull that image off, but the only person she's fooling is herself. I remember, she wore far too much make-up to cover up marks on her face and bad skin. And she looked and acted quite masculine. When I first met her, I thought she was a lesbian or drag queen. She's just got that look and way about her. And based on some of the stories Christopher told me, she acted very manly at times. I remember, he confided in me that she actually attacked him once. Given my poor boy was such a gentlemen, all he could do was restrain her until she'd calmed down because he would never have hit a woman. I raised him better than that."

Jane looked at Ethan and winced. "Well, she sounds like a bundle of joy."

"I did tell you she's a nasty piece of work."

Sylvia cleared her throat, no doubt to attract Jane and Ethan's attention. "Why are you asking me about her, anyway?"

"Well, a woman called Marlene may be attending the funeral tomorrow on behalf of her new boyfriend, Desmond, who supposedly dealt the fatal blow to Christopher. Ethan and I have no idea if it's the Marlene that Christopher had a relationship with, but if it is, then I'd certainly like to meet her."

Sylvia shook her head and blew out air. "Jane. That's asking a lot of me. I told Christopher I never wanted to meet her again, and I'm telling you the same thing."

Ethan raised his hand and interjected. "Sylvia. As Jane said, we don't know if it is *the Marlene*. But if it is, you don't have to talk to her. Jane and I will, but you don't have to."

"And, Sylvia," Jane said. "If it is *the Marlene* and she's held a grudge against Christopher since he left her for Ethan, she could be one of the suspects."

Sylvia shook her head vigorously and held her hands out to her side. "Okay. I concede. If you think she might be one of the suspects, then I suppose I have no choice but to let her attend if she decides to turn up. I swear to God though, if it turns out to be her who killed my boy, then I'll personally take it upon myself to make sure that justice is served and in my way."

"Well, the less you tell me about what that would be, the better, Sylvia. It could put me in a very compromising position if something odd or sinister happened to her."

"I appreciate that, Jane, so I'll spare you the gruesome details."

"That's great. And it may not even be the Marlene you met. But it does seem a bit coincidental that a woman called Marlene is now in a relationship with the person who the pathologist's report states was responsible for Christopher's death."

"Yes, it does sound very coincidental, so I'd better brace myself for the reality of seeing her again, and at my son's funeral. I honestly didn't think things could get any worse, but they just have."

Jane opened her mouth to speak when she heard the clanking of china behind her. She turned around, and Patricia had entered the room.

"Tea's here. Have I missed much?"

Sylvia looked toward Patricia. "I'll fill you in on the details when Ethan and Jane have left."

"Okay, that's fine." Patricia placed the tray she was carrying on the coffee table in between the two sofas. "Do you all want me to serve?"

Sylvia nodded her head. "That would be lovely, if you could, my dear. My hands are trembling at the moment, so I'd probably spill the tea everywhere."

"Oh, dear. You'll have to fill me in later on what I've missed out on. I'm assuming it's something bad?"

"Bad enough," Sylvia replied. "But it can wait until later. I'm just a little shaken up at the moment."

"Well, have a nice cup of tea and try to calm yourself down, dear."

While they were drinking their tea, Patricia had the opportunity to talk about her fond memories of Christopher and gave Jane a useful insight into Christopher's character, traits, and personality. Once they'd finished their tea, Sylvia led them down to the TV lounge in the basement where they watched video footage of Christopher with Sylvia and his father for just over an hour.

After speaking to Sylvia and Patricia and watching the video footage, Jane was beginning to get a good feel for who Christopher had been, the emotional turmoil he'd been through when he was growing up and then coming to terms with his sexuality.

Once they'd watched all the video footage Sylvia had sorted out, Ethan and Jane went back to Ethan's house and watched the video footage of when he and Christopher had been on holiday together, were at parties, and generally fooling around at their house when they were on their own.

It was evident and endearing to see how very much in love they'd been and the afternoon had helped Jane not only feel she knew who Christopher had been but to empathise with the pain and suffering Ethan and Sylvia must have been enduring.

As she walked to her car, she looked at her watch, and it was gone six. Jane called her husband to let him know she was about to drive home and that she'd see him in about forty minutes. He told her that he'd made dinner for them both and he'd wait until she got home before he ate.

All she longed to do was have something to eat and then have a nice relaxing bath. She felt physically and mentally drained after such a long and intense day. Despite the fact she was no closer to finding out who Christopher's killer was, she assured herself that things would become a lot clearer during and after the funeral.

CHAPTER ELEVEN

The funeral procession wasn't due to leave Sylvia's house until 3:15 in the afternoon, so Jane decided to spend the morning catching up on her e-mails. While she thought about her response to the first e-mail she had to deal with, she gazed out of the window, looked at her garden, and she was pleased to see it was a pleasant day. The sun was shining, and despite a few white puffy clouds floating by, it looked as though the weather would stay dry for Christopher's funeral.

Once she'd dealt with the most important e-mails, Jane called Robert to give him an update on what she'd found out and told him if she had time after the funeral and wake, she was going to the warehouse where the fight had taken place. It was the scene of the crime so she needed to see if she could unearth any other clues or evidence. Robert insisted she sent him an e-mail with the details of where the funeral was being held and where the warehouse was, just in case she needed some backup or anything untoward happened to her.

Once she'd sent the e-mail to Robert, she looked at her watch and reminded herself she had to go to the dry-cleaners to pick up her smart black trouser suit and charcoal grey silk blouse that she'd arranged to have cleaned. She went to the garage and put the bolt and wire cutters in the boot of her car. She wanted to do that before she got showered and dressed to avoid the risk of getting any marks on her nice clean clothes.

When she got back from the dry-cleaners, Jane made herself some lunch, and once it had settled and digested, she had a shower, blow-dried her hair, put her make-up on and got dressed.

By the time she'd finished, it was almost time for her to leave her house and drive to Sylvia's. She did a last-minute check that she had everything she needed, which included handcuffs, pepper spray and a collapsible metal baton. She didn't know what she was going to be confronted with when she met the suspects so she thought it was best to take as many precautions as she could.

As she drove to Sylvia's house, Jane went over the questions she'd planned to ask the suspects to reassure herself they wouldn't come across as being too interrogative or arouse any suspicion. If she was going to pretend that she was Christopher's aunt, she was limited on what she could ask the suspects and hoped what they said to her, and their body language would save her from having to ask any of them too many questions.

When she arrived at Sylvia's house, she let out a sigh of relief when she saw Ethan, Sylvia, and Patricia standing on the paved terrace at the front of the house. The area directly outside Sylvia's house had cones on the street spaced out every few metres for twenty metres, clearly strategically placed so that nobody could park there and prevent the horse-drawn carriage and funeral cars from stopping at the front of the house. Jane continued to drive along the road until she found a parking space.

As she approached the house, Ethan acknowledged her with a wave. She looked at the other small groups of people who were talking and wondered who was who. More particularly, if any of them were Dan, Mike, or Marlene. There was no sign of a tall blonde woman who remotely resembled Marlene, so Jane assumed she either wasn't going to attend or was only going to the cemetery.

As she walked along the pathway toward Ethan, Sylvia,

and Patricia, Jane did her best to remain as expressionless as possible and politely nodded at the people she passed who acknowledged her arrival.

Sylvia and Patricia were both wearing black veils, so Jane greeted them with an air kiss on either side of their faces and gently placed a hand on their forearms. She hoped those simple gestures would create the impression for any onlookers that there was a genuine family connection and bond. She then greeted Ethan in the same way.

Jane looked at Sylvia and sensed from her tightly pursed lips and the twitching in the creases of her mouth and jaw that she was fighting back a torrent of anger and emotion.

The four of them stood in silence as people approached them to offer them their condolences. Ethan, Patricia and Jane offered some words of thanks, but Sylvia remained silent and simply nodded her head.

After a few minutes, Ethan nudged Jane and leaned into her ear. "Shall we go inside for a moment so we can talk?" Jane looked at Ethan and nodded.

Ethan put a hand on Sylvia's forearm, and she abruptly turned to look at him. "Jane and I are going inside for a bit to have a chat." Sylvia nodded and turned her head to stare aimlessly at the front gate and street again. Jane suspected she was dreading the moment when the funeral cars arrived because seeing Christopher in a coffin would make his death seem so final.

Ethan led the way to the TV lounge in the basement. When they'd entered, he turned to Jane and sighed. "I thought we'd have more privacy down here, and we won't be overheard by anybody."

"It's probably the best place. So my burning question is, are Dan and Mike here yet?"

"Not yet. The people outside are neighbours who've come to pay their last respects. Sylvia made it clear to them they could come to watch the funeral procession leave, but the ceremony is going to be a very small and private affair."

"Okay, that's good. I didn't see any sign of Marlene, so we'll have to wait and see if she turns up."

"Yes, I'm sure Sylvia would have told me if she'd seen her here. My question is, when do you want me to introduce you to Dan and Mike? When they arrive, they'll probably say hello and offer their condolences, but it all seems a bit tense and uncomfortable to introduce you to them when they arrive."

"No. I agree. I think it'll be better to introduce me to them after the ceremony. Hopefully, everybody will be a bit more relaxed once that's over."

"Agreed. Although I'm not sure Sylvia is going to relax at any point today. She's extremely uptight and finding all this a lot harder to deal with than she'd expected."

"Do you think she'll crack and start attacking or making accusations against the suspects?"

Ethan clenched his teeth and shrugged his shoulders. "At this point, based on Sylvia's emotional state, anything could happen. I think both of us need to keep a close eye on her and do our best to keep the suspects away from her as much as possible, especially Marlene, if she turns up."

"We can only do our best, and I don't want to cause Sylvia any more duress by telling her to be strong and that it will all be over soon."

"No. Neither do I. All we can hope is that she remains strong and continues to keep her mouth shut."

"Agreed. Right, shall we get back out there? As you said, we need to keep a watchful eye on her."

Jane and Ethan joined the growing number of mourners. As two men, one of which looked to be in his early forties and the other in his early sixties, walked through the entrance gate and along the pathway, Ethan nudged Jane and leaned into her ear. "Here they come . . . Dan and Mike."

119

Jane nodded and focused on Dan and Mike as they approached them. The hairs on her forearms stood on end as she braced herself to meet two of the prime suspects.

They walked toward Ethan and greeted him. When he introduced Sylvia as Christopher's mother and Patricia and Jane as his aunts, they both dipped their heads and offered their condolences to them all.

To avoid a potentially awkward situation, Ethan looked at Dan and then Mike. "Shall we go and have a little chat, guys?"

Dan and Mike nodded their heads and then dipped their heads at Sylvia, Patricia and Jane. Ethan led them to a corner of the front garden where there were no people.

Ethan looked at Dan and Mike and blew out air. "Look, guys, I know this is a bit awkward for you both, but as you can probably see, Christopher's mother is absolutely distraught at the moment so I'm sure you both want to offer her more personal condolences, but I don't think this is the right time or place. She hasn't said a word all day, and I'm not sure anyone will get a word out of her today, and that includes me."

Dan put a hand on Ethan's shoulder and nodded. "That's fine, Ethan, and it's completely understandable. Sylvia may know who we are, even though we've never met her, and I suspect we're the last people she wants to speak to right now given Christopher lost his life while he was fighting. I'm sure she holds both of us partly responsible in some way. Me for training him, and Mike for not preventing it from happening."

"Thanks, Dan. I appreciate your understanding."

"Yeah. The same goes for me," Mike stated. "I hope she doesn't hold me responsible because I didn't feel comfortable coming here for that reason, but given you and Dan insisted,

I felt obliged to come. If at any point Sylvia tells you our presence is disturbing her, then please let us know. I can imagine what she's going through right now." Mike glared at Dan. "I know what it feels like to lose a son. Mine may not be dead, but he might just as well be."

Dan looked down at Mike and held his hands out to his side. "Come on, Mike. This isn't the time or place to bring that up."

"Yeah, I'm sorry, I know. Today isn't about my son, is it? It's about *your son,* isn't it?"

"Okay, guys. I have no idea what you're referring to, but today is not the day to grind axes about things that may have happened between you two in the past."

"I'm sorry, Ethan, and I apologise. I suppose being here has brought back some painful memories for me, but I need to put those to one side for today."

"Thank you, Mike. It's going to be a hard day for all of us, so the less difficult we can make it for Sylvia and her family, the better."

"Agreed," Dan stated.

"Okay, just to confirm, you're both in the second car. I'm afraid Sylvia has insisted on there being only family and me in the first car. I'm sorry, Dan because I know Christopher was like a son to you, and you were a part of his family, but Sylvia is adamant it should be me and Christopher's direct family in the first car."

"That's not a problem, Ethan. Maybe one day Sylvia will acknowledge the special relationship Christopher and I had, but I'm more than happy to respect her wishes and go in the second car."

"Thanks, Dan. I knew you'd understand." Ethan looked at his watch. "Right, guys, I'd better get back to Sylvia. The carriage and cars should be arriving very soon. If I don't get to speak to you sooner, I'll catch up with you both at the wake.

I'm assuming you're both coming back here after the ceremony?"

Dan looked at Mike. "Well, I'm certainly planning to come back here. What about you, Mike?"

Mike looked down at the ground and sighed. He looked up at Ethan and winced. "Ethan, if you don't mind, I'd rather not. It's been difficult enough for me to come here and attend the service, let alone come back and talk to people at the wake. I don't want people pointing the finger at me and blaming me for Christopher's death. I'd never live it down."

"I'm sure people wouldn't do that, but I can understand your reasons for not wanting to come back, and it's fine. Anyway, I'd better get back to Sylvia."

Mike and Dan tipped their heads, and Ethan turned to walk toward Sylvia. As he approached, Jane and Patricia looked in his direction, but Sylvia's glance remained fixed on the front gate. Ethan did his best to force a closed smile as he walked past people, but he suspected his face made his inner feelings and thoughts as transparent as water.

Ethan took his place beside Sylvia, and she linked her arm around Ethan's arm, so he raised it until it was at a right angle. The hushed murmurs surrounding them gradually stopped as the sound of horse's hooves clip-clopping on tarmac filled the warm afternoon air. They were followed by the gentle humming of car engines. The moment that Ethan, Sylvia, and Patricia had been dreading had arrived.

Sylvia gripped Ethan's arm tighter, and even though Ethan had seen Christopher dead in the mortuary, he swallowed hard as he tried to brace himself for when Christopher's coffin came into sight.

Within seconds two beautifully groomed white horses came into sight, and then Ethan's gaze was fixed on the carriage they were pulling. The funeral directors had done a superb job of arranging the wreaths around the coffin, but that was little or no consolation for Ethan because the love of his life was lying dead inside it.

Ethan's gaze was broken when he felt something pulling on his arm. He looked to his left and Sylvia was on the verge of collapsing. Her legs had given way on her so he quickly put his right hand on her arm, released his left arm from her grip and put it around her waist so he could better support her.

Ethan turned to Jane. "Jane, can you go around the other side and help prop her up. I think she may pass out."

"Of course." Jane ran to the other side of Sylvia and took her arm with her left hand. Once Patricia could see that Jane had hold of her, she released her grip and moved to the side so Jane could stand beside her. Jane looked at Ethan and mouthed, *I have smelling salts in my bag if she does pass out.*

Ethan nodded and mouthed back, *let's hope we won't need to use them, but it's good to know, just in case.* Ethan leaned into Sylvia's ear and whispered, "Sylvia, are you sure you can do this? It's not a problem if you want to go inside for a while until you feel better."

Sylvia shook her head. "I'm fine," she whispered. "Please just help me get to the car and don't let go of me while we're walking."

"Of course. Jane and I will make sure we get you to the car safely."

Once the horse-drawn carriage and limousines had stopped outside the front of the house, and the ushers had opened the doors, Sylvia took a hesitant step forward. "Come on. It's time for us to go."

Ethan looked at Jane and nodded. Ethan and Jane let Sylvia dictate the pace at which they walked, and Ethan tightened his hold on Sylvia's arm and waist. The garden path had never looked so long or been so uninviting as they walked at a snail's pace with their gazes fixed on the coffin in front of them.

Sylvia's whole body trembled as she tried to accept what she saw in front of her. Being told that Christopher had been killed had been torturous enough, but having to stare at a coffin with her dead son in it was overbearing. She wished she was just having a bad nightmare and that she'd wake up from it soon, but the reality was staring her straight in the face. She was wide awake and looking at her beloved son's coffin.

Even though Ethan and Jane tried guiding her toward the limousine behind the carriage, she resisted and guided them to the carriage. She wanted to look at the coffin so the realisation of having lost her son might finally sink in.

As she stared at the coffin and visions of Christopher flashed through her mind, she wanted to scream out loud and cry until there were no more tears left to cry. The one and only thing that stopped her from doing that was the anger and bitterness she felt toward the person or people who were responsible for killing her son. One of them could have been yards away from her, and she refused to give them the satisfaction of her tears.

She wanted revenge, and she owed it to her son to be strong until they'd found out who'd killed him. She consoled herself that then she'd be able to grieve, but in the meantime, she had to be strong for her son and suppress her inner emotions and feelings. She wasn't sure how she was going to be able to manage it, but she knew she had to find inner strength from somewhere. Nobody could bring her son back so whoever had been responsible for taking him away from her would pay a dear price for doing so.

As she contemplated how she would like to see them suffer in the most agonising and inhuman ways, her train of thought was broken when she felt someone breathing by her ear. She turned to her right.

"Are you ready to get in the car now, Sylvia?" Ethan asked.

Sylvia gently nodded her head and looked toward the limousine. She knew she'd have plenty of time to plan her revenge once the service was over and she was left alone with only a bottle of wine or sherry for company. Then her mind would really get to work and plan everything she needed to plan.

Jane stepped into the car first and put out a hand. Sylvia took hold of Jane's hand, and with Ethan's help, she managed to get into the car without stumbling or falling. Jane guided her to the back seat, and she sat down. Jane sat to the far left-hand side, allowing Patricia and Ethan to sit either side of her.

Even though Sylvia hadn't known Jane for long, she had a gut feeling she would get to the bottom of who'd killed her son, and that gave her great satisfaction — the only satisfaction she could derive from such a sad and tragic moment. As she stared at Christopher's coffin in front of her, she knew that would be her number one priority for now and the foreseeable future, and she was going to do her very best to maintain control throughout the day so that Jane had the opportunity to do her job.

She was determined not to make any accusations and be as polite as she could be to the suspects, even though she wanted to throw acid in their faces, cover them in petrol, light a match, and watch them burn in Hell on Earth.

Once all the guests and suspects were in the second car, the usher prompted the horses to start walking, and the cars began to follow. As Sylvia looked out of the window to her right, the neighbours were standing on the pavement watching as the funeral procession left the house.

When they were out of the neighbours' sights, Sylvia cleared her throat. "I must apologise to all three of you for hardly saying anything earlier. I just didn't want to encourage anybody to talk to me, and if I'm honest, while we were waiting for the coffin to arrive, I was incapable of speaking. I had a horrid lump in my throat, and at times, I thought I was going to choke on it."

Patricia squeezed Sylvia's arm. "Darling, there's no need to apologise to any of us. This is an extremely hard day for you, so none of us will be offended. You're doing great so far, so try to remain strong and remind yourself why we're doing this."

Sylvia bulked. "How could I forget?" She turned to Jane. "I hope today helps you discover who killed my son because knowing his murderer is probably here is killing me."

Jane gave her what looked like a forced, closed smile. "Until I meet the suspects and talk to them, I can't offer you any guarantees, but I'm pretty certain it'll lead me one step closer to finding out who did it."

"Well, I can ask for no more than that. Let's talk at the end of the day, and you can let me know what your thoughts or suspicions are."

"Of course. I hate to ask this right now, but did you see Marlene at your house?"

Sylvia gently shook her head. "No, I didn't see her. In some ways, I'm glad, but in other ways, I'm hoping she'll be at the cemetery, so you have the chance to talk to her."

"Well, we'll soon find out, but for now, you just focus on paying your last respects to your son."

Sylvia reached into her handbag, took out a handkerchief and discretely lifted it under her veil. Just hearing Jane say those words were as painful as any dagger could be—having to pay her last respects to her son. She dabbed her eyes to soak up the tears that burned as they streamed from her eyes. She'd managed to conceal her emotions up until that point, but just the thought of having to pay her last respects to her son made it seem all the more real and final.

Chapter Twelve

A s they drove through the grounds of the cemetery, seeing all the aged and weather-stained grave stones passing them by, reminded Jane of all her losses. The loved ones she'd had to say goodbye to, and her heart went out to Sylvia. Jane had never lost a son, but she had said goodbye to many close relations and just thinking about them made her feel emotional — something that would probably stand her in well when she spoke to the suspects after the ceremony.

The carriage and cars stopped by the side of a family plot, and Jane could see that one of the plots had been prepared for what she assumed was Christopher's burial. Standing about twenty feet away from the plot, Jane saw a tall blonde woman standing beside a tree, and she hoped her guess was right — that she was Marlene.

She didn't have to guess for long. Sylvia turned to her and nodded. "Well, there she is, Jane. In all her fine glory — not!"

"So, that's Marlene?"

"It certainly is. I'll never forget that face for as long as I live. That's her all right. I wonder if she'll have the courage to actually join us while the ceremony takes place."

"Jane and I will find a way to talk to her, Sylvia, so don't worry about that. And we'll keep her as far away from you as we can."

"That would be much appreciated, my dear."

They all got out of the car. Ethan approached Dan and Mike, said a few words to them, and they walked toward the carriage. Ethan's and Christopher's friends joined them, and

Jane assumed that Ethan had arranged for the six of them to carry the coffin to the plot.

As the coffin was pulled out of the carriage, Mike and three of the friends gripped the handles at the back end, and Ethan and Dan took the front end. Once they all had a firm hold on the handles, in unison, they took the full weight of the coffin and started walking toward the plot. Sylvia, Patricia and Jane followed behind them, and the other mourners followed them.

When they arrived at the plot, the six men placed the coffin on top of the casket lowering device. Sylvia led the way to one side of the coffin, and Jane and Patricia followed her lead. Ethan indicated to the other mourners they should stand at the other side of the coffin.

From where she was standing, Jane could see Marlene in the distance and wondered if she would come any closer, or if she intended to remain as inconspicuous as she could by staying at a safe distance where people wouldn't even acknowledge her presence. She hoped once the service had begun, she'd discretely move closer without drawing attention to herself. Jane wanted to talk to her before she had the opportunity to make a quick exit.

Jane leaned into Ethan. "It looks like she's going to stay where she is."

"Leave it with me." Ethan leaned into Sylvia and whispered, "Sylvia, I know this is going to be hard for you, but please, beckon Marlene to come and join us."

Jane expected Sylvia to ignore his request, but much to her pleasant surprise, Sylvia turned to Marlene, raised her hand and beckoned her to join them. Marlene paused for a few seconds and then started to walk toward them.

Jane wanted to give Sylvia a medal for her bravery and then a huge hug, but she knew that neither token gesture would be welcomed at that particular moment in time.

Content that she and Ethan would get the opportunity to talk to Marlene after the service, Jane tuned into what the minister was saying. He gave a very moving and touching speech that focused on who Christopher had been when he was alive, and Jane was relieved they didn't mention anything to do with how Christopher lost his life. She assumed Sylvia and Ethan had carefully briefed the minister on what to say, and what not to say.

At the end of the service, the coffin started to descend into the ground, and she didn't need to look at Sylvia, Ethan and Patricia, because she could hear their sniffling and yelps of sorrow as Christopher's body was laid to rest.

Although she didn't want to over-exaggerate, Jane took a tissue out of her bag and dabbed her eyes. She drew on her memories of when she'd had to say goodbye to her loved ones, so it stirred up her emotions and made her look like a convincing aunt who was grieving the loss of her beloved nephew.

As she looked at Dan, Mike,. and Marlene on the other side of the coffin, Dan was wiping tears away from his eyes, but Mike and Marlene were expressionless — void of any compassion or loss.

Once the service was over, Jane tugged on Ethan's arm and leaned into him. "It's time for you to introduce me to the suspects. Marlene first. I want to talk to her before she decides to leave."

"Follow me. Hold onto my arm."

Jane did as she was told, and they walked toward Dan, Mike, and Marlene who were stood next to each other in a closed group. As they approached, Ethan coughed, no doubt to announce their arrival. Dan and Mike stood to one side so Jane and Ethan could join the group. Marlene stayed where she was, and her gaze flitted backward and forward to Jane and Ethan.

Ethan looked at the three suspects and held his hands out. "I hope you'll forgive the intrusion, but I wanted to say thank you to all of you, especially you, Marlene, for making the effort to come and say your final farewells to Christopher. We all appreciate it."

Marlene looked down at Ethan with pursed lips and gently nodded her head. "Well, hello, Ethan. At last, we finally get to meet in person. I've seen you at the ringside with Dan and Christopher on a number of occasions, so I'm assuming you're Ethan? The man who stole my man from me?"

Ethan looked down at the ground and Jane could see he was biting his lip, so she decided to step in. "Okay, Marlene, I don't think this is the time or the place for that kind of talk. Please respect where we are and why we're here."

Marlene looked down at Jane and sneered. "Oh, excuse me, miss prim and proper. And who might you be?"

Jane sighed and glared at Marlene. "Well, if you were that close to Christopher, I thought you'd have known that I was his aunt, Jane."

Marlene cupped her chin with her hand, nodded her head and frowned. "Hum. Let me think. Maybe he did mention you a couple of times, but he never showed me a photo of you. It was a long time ago, so maybe my memory's failing me. I remember him talking about his aunty Patricia, but I don't remember him talking about you so much."

"Hmm. That might be because I live in Whitstable in Kent, so we were a bit distant. We used to talk on the phone quite often, but in retrospect, perhaps not as often as we should have done."

"Yeah, well, if I'm perfectly honest, and no offence, Ethan, but I came here for the sake of my boyfriend, Desmond, as opposed to Christopher."

Jane looked at Ethan with an open mouth and wide eyes. When Ethan didn't say anything, Jane decided it was up to her to deal with Marlene. It was clearly beyond Ethan's capabilities. "Okay, so putting your obvious charm and diplomacy to one side, why exactly did you come here?"

Marlene sniggered, looked around at the other people who'd attended the ceremony and then fixed her gaze on Jane. "To see what rumours people are spreading about my boyfriend. And if I hear one person dissing him, or dragging his name through the dirt, then I'm gonna pull them up on it."

"Why! Aren't you the charm—" Jane was stopped in her tracks when the vision of the apparition, Ricky, appeared standing between Marlene and Mike. Her mouth opened as she watched the haunting silhouette of his figure grab his throat with his hands and began to cough. Her wide eyes followed him as he dropped to his knees and laid still.

Jane covered her mouth with her hand and gasped. The apparition had indicated that Christopher's death had something to do with either Marlene or Mike. Or at least she thought that's what he'd tried to indicate.

A muffled voice brought Jane back to her senses. "Are you all right, Jane?" Dan asked.

Jane looked up and tried to disguise her shock, but secret delight. "Oh, yes. Forgive me. I'm prone to have funny spells now and again, and I think with all the emotion of today, I was just hit with one."

"Okay, so long as you're sure. Blimey, it looked like you'd seen a ghost."

Jane chuckled and waved a hand in the air. "Oh, don't be silly. Ghosts don't exist, do they?"

"Not that I know of," Ethan commented.

"Anyway, Jane, what were you about to say about me?" Marlene asked in a stroppy manner.

"I was going to say aren't you the charming one. I appreciate you may have come here with your own agenda, but there was no need to make it so apparent to Ethan, or any of us come to that matter."

Marlene laughed mockingly. "Yeah, well, I tell it how it is. There's no point in lying or beating around the bush, is there?"

"All right, Marlene," Dan interjected. "I've heard enough of your nonsense for one day. Be respectful or leave now."

Marlene looked at Dan and snarled. "So who are you now? My father, or what?"

"I tell ya what. If you carry on the way you are, I won't hesitate to put you over my knee and give you the good spanking you deserve."

Marlene glared at Dan. Her body tensed, and she held her hands out to the side and clenched her fists. "Don't you think you're a bit too old and past it to try and lay a hand on me?"

Dan leaned into Marlene, clenched his fist and tapped it against Marlene's jaw. "You just carry on, young lady, and I'll show you exactly what I'm still capable of."

"Yeah, yeah, yeah, big talker. I'd knock you out in one round."

"Will the two of you shut up, please," Ethan pleaded. "I'm not having any of that fighting talk at Christopher's funeral. It's almost time for us to leave and go back to the wake at Sylvia's house. Dan, are you still coming?"

"Yes, of course I am."

"Mike, have you changed your mind?"

"Yeah. Dan's convinced me I should go, and nobody's made me feel uncomfortable, so yeah, count me in."

Ethan looked at Marlene. "And you, Marlene. Are you coming?"

"Hmm, that depends on whether I'm invited or not. I can't imagine for one minute Sylvia wants me to be there, but if she invites me personally, then I'll come back."

Ethan covered his face with his hands and sighed heavily.

After a couple of seconds, he looked up at Marlene and held his hands out to his side. "I'll do what I can, but on this occasion, I think you might be right."

"Well, there's only one way to find out, and that's to go and talk to her. I'll wait here for you, little man."

Jane looked at Marlene and shook her head. "Come on, Ethan. Let's go and talk to Sylvia. I think I've heard enough from her for the time being."

Jane took hold of Ethan's arm and steered him toward Sylvia. "Gees, I know you and Sylvia said she was a bitch, but she's way surpassed my expectations of how bitchy a woman can be. I wanted to knock her out there and then. The disrespectful cow. But if you can convince Sylvia to invite her, I have a plan."

Ethan turned to look at Jane. "And what's that? And what just happened back there? You did see a ghost, didn't you?"

"Yep. The very same druggy who's paid me a couple of visits before."

"So, what happened?"

"He stood in between Marlene and Mike and re-enacted what happened to Christopher."

"Blimey, so do you think he was trying to tell you that Marlene and Mike are responsible for Christopher's death?"

"It's very probable, but I have a plan to find out if it's true."

"And what's that?"

"I'm going to make my excuses for leaving the wake early because I want to go to the warehouse where Christopher was killed before I drive back home. And I'm going to tell you when you're talking to the three of them. If one of them is responsible, I have a sneaky feeling that whoever did it will follow me there. They won't want me snooping around the warehouse, so I'm sure it'll provoke a reaction."

"Are you sure about this, Jane? It could be dangerous, especially if two of them turn up."

Jane tugged on Ethan's arm gently and looked at him. "Hey, I don't think it's Dan, so even if Marlene and Mike do turn up, I think I can handle both of them. I can't imagine Mike fighting anybody. He's too old and unfit. Besides, I have a few little accessories in my bag that I can resort to if the need arises." Jane winked at Ethan and smiled.

Ethan looked at Jane and blew out air. "All right, so long as you're sure. I trust your judgement, so go for it. If I'm honest, my head feels so groggy, and I know I have to get through the rest of the day without losing sense of my emotions so I'll leave it in your capable hands."

"You do that. I'm pretty confident that what I've planned will provoke the reaction I want."

When they reached Sylvia and Patricia who were standing on their own, Jane and Ethan stood in front of them. Ethan put a hand on Sylvia's hand and took a deep breath. "Hi, Sylvia, how are you coping?"

"I'm still managing to keep it together, but what happens next? Did you get any clues while you were talking to those three?"

Ethan nodded and put both his hands on Sylvia's hand. "We think so. And Jane has a plan to find out if the apparition she just saw gave her the clue she's been waiting for."

"Oh, good. That sounds very encouraging." Sylvia's glassy blue bloodshot eyes were fixed on Jane's. "Well, whatever your plan is, Jane, I hope it works."

"I'm reasonably confident it will . . . but there's one thing you have to do to help me execute my plan."

"Name it, and I'll do it. I'm beyond my own grief right now, and all I can think about is finding out who killed my son so justice can be served."

"You're not going to like what you have to do," Ethan interjected.

"I'm not liking anything about today, so please, just tell me what I have to do, and I'll do it. I'm on a mission now, and if Jane has a plan, I want it to be executed. Just like the person or people who killed my son."

Ethan looked at Jane and winced. Jane nodded and looked at Sylvia. "It means you'll have to invite Marlene back to your place for the wake."

Sylvia took a deep breath and sighed. "That's a tall order, but if that's what you need me to do, then I'll do it. But I'll say nothing more to her. I'll invite her back to the wake, and then I'm going to the car."

Jane put a hand on Sylvia's hand and smiled. "Thank you, Sylvia. I appreciate how difficult this must be for you, but please trust me. I will find the person or people who are responsible for Christopher's death. I've never let a client down before, and I certainly have no intention of letting you down."

Sylvia looked at Jane and forced a closed smile. She squeezed Janes hand and nodded. "Come on. Let's get this over and done with before I change my mind."

Sylvia stuck to her word but very diplomatically avoided having to invite Marlene personally back to the wake. She just walked up to the three suspects and said she looked forward to seeing all of them at her place.

As they drove back to Sylvia's house, Jane took the time to think through the finer details of her plan, and how she was going to execute it to perfection. She had started to feel for Ethan and Sylvia on a personal level for their loss, and she was more determined than ever to make sure that her plan worked out exactly as she'd planned it.

CHAPTER THIRTEEN

As Sylvia approached the front door to her house, she reached into her handbag and searched for her key holder. She took it out, opened it and found the key to open the front door. As she tried to put the key in the lock, her hand trembled so much she struggled to put the key in it. Patricia obviously noticed she was struggling, took the key out of her hand and opened the door. Sylvia went to the keypad for the alarm and tapped in the code.

Her mind was filled with a mixture of horror, knowing she was most probably allowing Christopher's killer into her house, and concern that the caterers hadn't set up the marquee and organised the buffet and refreshments. She walked through the reception room with Patricia at her side and headed toward the kitchen where they were greeted by one of Sylvia's trusted neighbours, Elizabeth, and two of the servers.

Elizabeth looked at Sylvia, walked toward her, and put a hand on her forearm. "How did it go, my dear?"

"As well as can be expected, but I'll be extremely pleased when today is over."

"I can imagine, my dear. Well, everything is set up in the marquee as you requested, so hopefully, that's one less thing to concern yourself about. They've put on a lovely spread, so nobody will go hungry."

"Oh, please, don't talk to me about food at the moment. I'd probably wretch if I went outside and looked at it."

"That's understandable. Would you like me to make you

and Patricia a nice cup of tea?"

"That'd be lovely if it's not too much trouble."

"It'll be with you in a jiffy. You go and sit yourselves down, and I'll bring it over to you." Elizabeth walked toward the kettle and set about making the tea.

Ethan walked into the kitchen and guided the mourners into the garden. He quickly looked at Sylvia who was sitting at the kitchen table and mouthed *I'll be with you in a minute.*

Sylvia raised a hand to acknowledge she'd understood him.

Jane was talking to Dan as they passed through the kitchen, and Sylvia hoped she was working on her plan. Once everybody had gone out into the garden, Ethan joined her and Patricia at the table.

"How are you doing, Sylvia?"

"Hmm. That's why I wanted to talk to you. I think I'm going to have a cup of tea with Patricia and Elizabeth. Then I think I'll go up to my room and have a lie down. I feel absolutely exhausted after today, and I can feel a headache coming on, so I really don't want to be around people — especially the three suspects. I fear I might crack and say or do something I shouldn't. Neither of you mind, do you?"

Patricia put a hand on Sylvia's hand. "Of course not, dear. It'll do you good to get some rest. Ethan and I can take care of the people here."

"Of course not, Sylvia. I'll make your excuses for you, and I'm sure people will be more than understanding," Ethan stated reassuringly.

"You are a sweetie. So, do you think Jane's plan will work?"

"Well, we'll find out later on today. She's going to make it very public to the three suspects she wants to go to the warehouse before she drives back home. She's pretty convinced that whoever did it will follow her because they won't want her snooping around."

"Oh, what a smart thinking woman. I hope she'll be safe, though. I dread to think what those three might do to her if they find out who she really is."

"Well, she's assured me she's confident she can take care of herself, and with her background, I have every faith in her."

"Yes, I suppose you're right. Anyway, we can chat later. Here comes Elizabeth with the tea, and you should go and join the others before they start suspecting something."

"Okay, I'll talk to you later."

"If I'm still in bed, and you get some news from Jane, please be sure to come up and call me."

"Of course I will. You have my word."

Jane had deliberately asked Dan to tell her exactly what happened on the night of the fight. She'd heard Ethan's account and wanted to hear Dan's. As they stood together in the garden, Jane listened intently as Dan recounted everything she'd seen in the video, but she didn't tell Dan she'd seen the video. Once he'd finished telling her what happened, she nodded and covered her mouth with her hand.

After some reflective thought, Jane cupped her chin with her hand and looked at Dan with her head cocked to one side. "So, what about the pathologist's report? Do you believe Christopher was killed by a fatal blow to the head?"

Dan crossed his arms in front of him and looked around the garden. Jane took that as a sign that he wanted to avoid eye contact with her. He unfolded his arms, placed his hands together in front of his mouth and breathed out. "Well, I can only go on what the pathologist's report says, but if I find out it wasn't a fatal blow to his head that killed him, I'll be looking into what really happened."

"Well, if you do find out it was something other than a blow to his head, then please let me know. I wouldn't suggest telling Ethan or Sylvia because that's what they believe, so it's probably best to let them continue believing what they already do."

"Yeah, sure, and I agree. I think it'd destroy them more than it already has to discover Christopher died from a different cause."

"I agree. But I'm not so attached so you can let me know. Let me give you my mobile number."

"Sure. If I find anything out, I'll let you know."

Jane reached into her handbag and took out her purse. She gave Dan a business card with the name of a fictional arts and crafts shop in Whitstable with her mobile phone number on it. "There you go. Keep that safe and give me a call if you hear anything."

"Thanks. I'll put your number in my phone now just in case I lose your card. Arts and crafts, eh? You don't look or come across as being the type, especially after the way you spoke to Marlene. I thought she was going to blow a gasket and clock you one."

Jane looked at Dan and smiled sarcastically. "Well, you know what they say. You should never judge a book by its cover. Anyway, I suppose I'd better go and introduce myself to other people here. Otherwise, they'll think I'm very rude, and it doesn't look like Sylvia will be making an appearance, so I guess I should help fulfil her obligations."

"That's fine. No problem. Perhaps I'll see you a bit later?"

"Oh, I'm sure you will. I'll certainly say goodbye before I leave, and if you leave before me, then please come over and say goodbye."

"Sure. Right, well, I suppose I'm left with no other option but to go and talk to Mike and Marlene. I despise the woman, but given I don't know anybody else, I guess I have no other choice."

"Good luck. I can completely understand why you despise the woman. I despised her after talking to her for thirty seconds. She's not exactly a lady, and she's hard as nails from what I can make out."

"Trust me, you don't want to know what lies below in that warped, bizarre mind of hers."

"I'll take your word for that. Anyway, I'll catch up with you later. Ethan is on his way so we'll do the rounds and then come back to talk to you, Mike, and Marlene."

"Gotcha. See ya later."

Jane walked toward Ethan, and she put her hands out in front of her to stop him. She looked around to make sure that nobody was close to enough to hear them, and then turned to Ethan. "Okay. I've just had a chat with Dan, and I'm pretty convinced he had nothing to do with Christopher's death."

Ethan blew out air and held his hands out to his side. "So, what now?"

"I'll focus on the other two, but first I want you to introduce me to some other people. I want the suspects to see us circulating and mingling with the other people here so they don't start questioning why we're spending all our time with them."

Ethan nodded. "I get where you're coming from." He looked around and then focused his gaze on Jane. "Come on. I'll introduce you to Penelope and John, and Richard and George. We'll have a chat with them and then go back to Dan, Mike, and Marlene."

"Great. Let's do it." Jane turned, held onto Ethan's arm, and they walked toward the two couples.

They spent about twenty minutes talking together about their memories of Christopher and the fun times they'd had together. Jane made a contribution when she could relate it to something Ethan and Sylvia had told her or what she'd seen in the videos.

Jane looked at her watch, and it was a 5:45. She wanted to arrive at the warehouse while there was still natural light, so she cleared her throat to get Ethan's attention. "I'll have to make a move very soon, so I'm going to say goodbye to Dan, Mike, and Marlene."

"Okay, Jane, I'll accompany you."

As they walked toward the three suspects, Jane leaned into Ethan and whispered, "After some polite chit-chat, I'm going to drop my bombshell and see what the reaction is. Text or call me if any of the suspects follow me.

"Of course I will, and I wish you the best of luck."

As they approached, Marlene looked at them, leaned heavily on her right leg and crossed her arms in front of her chest. "Oh, how nice of you to grace us with your presence again." She glared at Jane. "I didn't think we'd be seeing you again after our last little chat."

"Well, you can drop your attitude, Marlene, because I'm literally here to say goodbye to you all. After Dan told me what happened at the fight, I want to pass by the warehouse where it took place so I can see where my nephew died before I head back home. That's where I feel I should be paying my last respects to him."

Mike's eyes widened, and he took in a gulp of air and breathed out heavily. "Ooh. Are you sure you really want to go there? It might cause more damage than good."

"Well, there's only one way to find out, isn't there?"

Marlene looked at Jane inquisitively and nodded her head gently. "Well, I'd be careful if I were you. It's a very isolated area, and we've already lost one person at that place. It'd be such a shame to lose another one."

"Marlene!"

"That's fine, Dan. As you know, I'm an arts and crafts specialist, so I'm sure I'll be able to take care of myself. And I only want to look at it from the outside. I just want to know where my nephew lost his life."

"Are you sure you don't want one of us to come with you?" Marlene asked sarcastically. "We don't want you getting all scared and upset on your own, and I don't think trying to protect yourself with a piece of paper or card is going to frighten off the rough little buggers who hang around in that place at night."

"Marlene . . . is there no end to your intolerance and bad attitude? I'll be fine on my own, and if it meant having your company on the journey, then I'll definitely be all right. Guys, I'll bid you both farewell." Jane glared at Marlene. "And you, young lady, I hope I never have the misfortune of meeting you again for as long as I live."

Marlene faked a smile and waved a hand at Jane. "The feeling is mutual. Bye!"

Dan looked at Jane and mouthed, *I'm sorry* and held his hands out to his side.

"Right, I'm off. Ethan, would you escort me to the door, please?"

"Of course. It'd be my pleasure."

As they walked, Jane's fury festered. She turned to Ethan and blew out air. "I tell you what. I so hope that Marlene's the one responsible for this because I want to knock the crap out of her. She has really wound me up, and I'm on fire now. Let me know if any of them follow me so I can prepare myself."

"Yeah, sure, but try to calm down a bit. I can see she's definitely got something in for you, so prepare yourself for a visitor because I think one of them is coming for you."

"Oh, don't you worry. I'm more prepared than ever now she's wound me up. I feel like I could take the world on at the moment."

"Okay, well, just be careful and call me if you need me."

"Don't worry, I will."

Jane left Sylvia's house and walked toward her car. When she got in it, she banged her clenched fists on the steering wheel several times. She was furious, and Marlene had taken it upon herself to pick a battle with her, and there was no way in the world she was going to back down—no matter how much taller and bigger she was.

As Jane focused on the roads ahead of her and referred to Ethan's directions, she started to calm down a bit, but there was still a rage inside her. Within a few minutes, her mobile phone indicated she'd received a message. She waited until she had to stop at a red light and read the message. *Marlene has left. She said she was going to the bathroom and hasn't come back. Be careful and call me later. Ethan.*

Jane chuckled to herself and tapped the steering wheel with her fingernails. "Oh, good. It's show time, and I'm gonna take that bitch down."

As she drove, Jane kept checking her rearview mirror, but she couldn't see any car that appeared to be following her. She concluded Marlene wouldn't have needed to follow her because she knew where the warehouse was so she'd probably taken a different route in an attempt to disguise the fact she had every intention of confronting Jane at the warehouse.

Jane hoped that in a very short while, she'd get to the bottom of who'd killed Christopher, and every indication to date pointed toward Marlene.

CHAPTER FOURTEEN

Jane arrived at the warehouse and gauged she had about ninety minutes of daylight left. She parked her car in front of the padlocked gates, got out and opened the boot of the car. She took the bolt cutters out, went to the gates and after a couple of attempts managed to cut through the thick metal chain that was meant to keep vandals and the public out.

Once she'd driven through the gates, she stopped the car, got out and walked back to the gates. She closed them and wrapped the chain around them to keep them closed so that nobody apart from Marlene would suspect she was there. She drove to the back of the warehouse, where Ethan had told her to go.

She noticed that unlike the main building, which had large rectangular windows, most of which had been broken by vandals, the windows that stretched along the back wall of the building were much smaller. She imagined they were the offices where the manager and clerical staff had worked when the warehouse had been operational. Judging by the poor condition it was in, she suspected it had been abandoned for at least ten years and wondered why it hadn't been knocked down for redevelopment or turned into trendy apartments given that seemed to be all the rage in central London.

Jane parked her car and looked at the backdoor entrance. She got out of the car and got her bolt cutters out of the boot. When she reached the door, she cut through the chain and pushed the door open, which prompted a scuttling sound in the distance. She flinched and paused as she tried to assess what had caused the noise. When something ran over her foot, she quickly looked down and huffed when she saw it was nothing more than a small grey rat.

Convinced the scuttling sound she'd heard were other rats, and they were probably the only living thing inside the warehouse, she focused on the task at hand. She looked up and ahead and saw nothing more than a bare brick wall in front of her, so she peered inside and to her right. Her nostrils filled with dusty musky air that was tinged with the smell of oxidised metal. The air was surprisingly cool considering it had been such a warm day.

There were faint streams of sunlight about every five metres shining through what Jane imagined to be doorways to the rooms at the back of the warehouse. As she focused on the entrance to the main warehouse at the end of the long narrow corridor, it appeared to be better illuminated, no doubt due to the much larger windows.

Not wanting to take any chances, Jane went back to her car, put the bolt croppers in the boot and grabbed her heavy-duty flashlight. She locked her car, walked back into the warehouse and cautiously walked along the corridor toward where the first stream of light was coming from. She held her flashlight out in front of her to guide her and use it as protection in the unlikely event somebody was hiding in the room and about to attack her.

As she approached the room, she edged her way over to the left-hand side of the corridor, so she had more time to react if somebody did run out of the room or lunged forward to hit her.

Once she'd reached the doorway, she apprehensively edged forward, keeping her left leg behind her and her right foot in front. It was her strongest defence position, and her right leg was in a good position to kick out and hit anybody who came toward her in the crotch or stomach.

Jane stopped when she heard the rustling of what sounded like dry paper. "Is there anybody in here?" she called out. When there was no response, she took another step forward, so her right hand was inside the room. Nobody tried to grab it so she hesitantly took another step forward until she could peer inside the room and check nobody was hiding behind the doorway. She quickly surveyed the room, and nobody appeared to be in it.

Jane breathed a sigh of relief and walked into the room. As she looked around, her ears were sensitive to any other noises she could hear in the distance—coming from any of the other rooms, the main warehouse and outside. She had no idea when Marlene would be arriving, so she had to work fast and constantly be on alert.

Once she'd reassured herself there was no evidence or clues in the first room, Jane moved onto the next room. Again, it was cleaner and less cluttered than she'd expected, but she concluded they were the rooms where the fighters got changed.

Feeling more comfortable there was nobody else in the warehouse with her, Jane hurriedly searched through the desk drawers, lockers, and filing cabinets in the room. Just when she was about to leave, the photocopier on top of a desk in the corner caught her attention.

Jane walked toward it and opened the compartment at the bottom, but it was full of the photocopiers working mechanism. She quickly opened the A4 paper tray at the top, and it was half full of soiled paper. When she opened the A3 paper compartment below it, her eyes widened, and she yelped with joy.

Staring her in the face were the shorts that Desmond had been wearing on the night of the fight. Whoever had put them there had carefully folded them so they'd snuggly fit into the paper tray—and who apart from Jane would think of looking in a paper tray?

Jane took a clean specimen bag and rubber glove out of her handbag. Once she'd put the glove on, she carefully folded the shorts, being careful not to touch the waistband. She put them in the specimen bag, sealed it and put it in her handbag.

Satisfied she had everything she needed to find out and convict whoever was responsible for Christopher's death, Jane quickly left the room and ran toward the main warehouse.

The cage was still in the centre of the warehouse and Jane walked toward it. She'd seen it in the video footage, but it seemed more menacing and intimidating being surrounded by an eerie silence and shrouded in hazy streams of sunlight.

Jane stepped into the cage and examined the floor. It was splattered and smeared with so many bloody stains that Jane suspected it would take a forensic team an eternity to find any relevant clues that would lead to the conviction of Christopher's murderer. She concluded that the best evidence she'd find was safely guarded in her handbag.

As she walked around the ring looking for any other clues, Jane heard the purring of a car engine outside, and it sounded as if the car was stationary. From the height of the cage floor, she could see through the windows, and it came as no surprise to see Marlene removing the chain from the entrance gates and pushing them open.

Jane nodded her head and clenched her fists. "It's showtime, and time to find out just how nasty that bitch can be."

Knowing she only had a matter of minutes before she was going to be confronted by Marlene, Jane went to her handbag and checked that everything was organised properly so she'd have access to everything she might need as quickly as possible. Content that it was, she took her jacket off, pulled her blouse out of her trousers a bit so that nothing restricted her movements, put her handbag on her shoulder and braced herself for Marlene's arrival.

The clicking of Marlene's high heels against the hard, concrete floor announced her arrival. Jane looked at the entrance to the warehouse where she'd entered and waited for her first glimpse of Marlene.

When Marlene entered the warehouse, she paused for a few seconds and fixed her gaze on Jane. She nodded her head and then took long, confident strides toward the cage. "Right, *Jane*, do you wanna start off by telling me who you really are and why you're here?"

Jane peered down at Marlene, leaned on her left leg and folded her arms in front of her chest. "Well, you know my story, so why don't we start off by you telling me *why you're here?*"

Marlene snorted and shook her head. "Ha! If you think I fell for that crock of shit you fed us all at the funeral and wake, then you've got another thing coming. I wasn't born yesterday, sweetheart. You ain't Christopher's aunt, that's for sure. If you were, he'd have told me about you, so come on . . . who the fuck are you?"

Jane cupped her chin with her hand and tapped her thumb against it. "Hmm. It's nice to see you've a foul mouth as well as a foul presence."

Marlene scowled and banged a foot on the floor. "Enough of the wisecracks, bitch. You're the fucking filth, ain't ya?"

Jane looked at Marlene quizzically and pushed her shoulders back. "The what?"

Marlene sniggered, took three steps forward and stood at the bottom of the steps that led up to the cage. "The filth . . . the police, a copper! That clear enough for ya?"

Jane chuckled and shook her head. "As clear as water, but I'm sorry to disappoint you because I'm none of those."

Marlene walked up the steps and entered the cage. She put her handbag down on the floor, pulled her shoes off and put them beside her handbag. "Well, if you ain't the filth, then who are ya, and why the fuck are you snooping around here?"

"I told you. I just wanted to see where Christopher lost his life."

"Yeah, all right, love, you ain't pulling the wool over my eyes that easily." Marlene pointed at Jane and snarled. "You'd better start telling me the truth, bitch, cos I'm getting fed up with all your bullshit. And if you don't tell me the truth, then . . ."

Jane cocked her head and laughed. "Then what, Marlene? I'm dying to know."

Marlene clenched her fists, pulled her left hand back and put her right hand out in front of her. "I'll beat it out of you, that's what, bitch."

Jane put her hands out to her side and shook her head. "So you'd hit a woman who's twice your age and half your size?"

Marlene took a step forward and leaned back on her left leg. "If you don't tell me who the fuck you are and what you're doing here, then yes."

"Why, aren't you the charming one?"

"Will you fuck off with all your stupid snobby comments and just tell me who the fuck you are, or . . ."

"I'll tell you when I'm good and ready. But before I do, I want to go back to my original question. What are you doing here? Got something to hide, Marlene?" Jane fixed her gaze on Marlene and smirked.

"What the fuck? Why would you think I've got something to hide? What ain't you telling me, bitch?"

Jane shrugged her shoulders and reached into her handbag. She pulled out the bag with Desmond's shorts in it and held it out in front of her. "Well, I just thought you might have followed me so you could reclaim these before I found them."

"You fucking bitch. You're a cop all right, and those shorts are leaving with me!"

"Oh, is that right? And what makes you think I'm just gonna hand them over to you?"

"By the time I've knocked you out, love, you won't need to hand them over to me. I'll just take them."

Jane chuckled, put the shorts back in her handbag and placed it on the floor beside her. "Well, you're pretty cock-sure of yourself, but what makes you think you'll be able to knock me out?" While Marlene had the upper hand on Jane when it came to size, she knew she had the upper hand when it came to the element of surprise. She doubted if Marlene remotely suspected Jane was a karate expert so she'd be in for a huge surprise when Jane defended herself and attacked — she was confident Marlene wouldn't be prepared for that.

Marlene laughed out loud and shook her head. "I tell ya what, darling, you're either stupid or mad. Look at ya. You wouldn't last two minutes with me. Do you know who I am?"

Jane fixed her gaze on Marlene's steely blue eyes, shrugged her shoulders and sighed. "Perfectly well, thanks."

Marlene pulled her head back and pursed her lips. "And you're not scared?"

"Why should I be?"

"You stroppy, condescending, bitch!" Marlene ran toward Jane with the force of a raging bull and anger shone brightly in her soulless and unforgiving eyes. When she was within arm's reach, Marlene swung a right hook with what Jane imagined was all her might, and it was headed straight toward her face.

Jane ducked and quickly stepped to her left. With lightning reactions, she glanced to her right to gauge where Marlene was. Marlene clearly hadn't expected Jane to dodge her punch because she'd stumbled forward slightly and her back and head were tilted forward.

Without hesitation, Jane seized her opportunity, clenched

her right fist and elbowed Marlene in the back as close as she could get to where her kidneys were. Marlene yelped, and her hands intuitively clasped her back.

Jane spun to her right and front kicked the back of Marlene's knee with her right leg. Marlene's leg buckled, and she put her hands out in front of her to break her fall.

Marlene quickly flipped her body around, looked up at Jane and hissed. "Okay. So there's clearly more to you than meets the eye. Nice one. I owe you that, but you won't be so lucky the next time."

Jane chuckled and shook her head. "You rely too much on your size and big mouth, sweetheart. I'd try focusing a bit harder and work on your reflexes if you're planning on coming at me again."

Marlene brushed herself down, stood up and glared at Jane. "You bet I'm coming for you again, and you'd better be ready for me."

Jane tutted and shook her head. "Whenever you're ready, babe, but can you hurry up . . . this is starting to get a bit boring. I expected a bit more from you given you act so tough."

"What the fuck? You'd better keep that stuck up little mouth of yours shut, or I'm gonna fill it."

"Well, darling, I know one thing for sure, it won't be your fist filling my mouth."

Marlene gritted her teeth, clenched her fists and stood in an attack position with both hands out in front of her. Jane raised her hands and bent her elbows, so they were at ninety-degree angles, and held her open hands out vertically in front of her, a body width apart. They were flat and in line with her chest, so she was prepared to block any punches that Marlene threw at her.

Marlene edged forward, and Jane spread her feet in line with her body. She was in the perfect defence position and ready to deal with anything Marlene came forward with.

After a few seconds, Marlene ran forward and raised her right knee, which indicated to Jane she was going to do a front kick. Jane's only concern was that she was going to change tactics and hop onto the other leg, twist her body and do a round kick to her head.

Marlene extended her leg in front of her and Jane anticipated what was coming. She side-stepped her foot to avoid it hitting her in the stomach, and when it had passed her body, she grabbed it with both hands and pushed it up.

Jane had hoped Marlene would lose her balance, but she hopped on her left leg to maintain it. Jane pushed her leg up higher so she could take a step forward and use Marlene's leg and her arms to block any punches that Marlene tried to hit her with.

Jane used her left leg to do an outside sweep on Marlene's left leg, and she was helpless to do anything else but topple and hit the cage floor with a thud. Marlene exhaled sharply and tried to recover her breath.

Seizing her moment, Jane forced Marlene's leg back further, and she yelped. Jane walked to the side of Marlene and stomped her foot on her stomach. When Marlene grabbed her stomach with both hands, Jane let go of her leg and ran to her handbag.

Jane grabbed the handcuffs, and when she started running back to Marlene, she was getting herself back onto her feet. Jane didn't stop running, and when she reached her, she turned to her side, put her weight on her left leg, bent her right knee and kicked out. She hit Marlene on the side of the head, and she screamed, placed a hand on her head and hit the cage floor with a loud thud.

A flock of pigeons that had taken nest in the old warehouse took to flight and the still air filled with the sound of flapping wings and squawks as they flew out of the broken windows or settled on the huge decaying metal beams that supported the roof and structure.

Once Marlene had obviously recovered from the shock and pain, she turned to Jane and snarled. "You fucking bitch. I'm gonna kill you!"

"Lovely. Glad to hear that and I'm glad to see you haven't lost your sense of humour."

Once again, Marlene made an attempt to clamber to her feet. Jane ran to the back of her and grabbed her hair with her free hand and started pulling it. Marlene's hands grabbed Jane's hand, and she tried to release Jane's grip.

"Thank you, darling. That's just where I wanted them." Jane placed one of the cuffs on Marlene's right wrist, closed it and gripped the chain connecting the two handcuffs. "Almost there, sweetheart. Not long now."

"What the fuck are you doing?"

"You'll find out soon enough. Now shut the fuck up and let me get on with my job!"

Marlene fumbled with the handcuff on her wrist, and when she'd obviously realised it was locked, she reached out for Jane's hands. Every time she did, Jane used one of her feet to kick her forearms, and clearly, Marlene wasn't as fond of, or couldn't take as much pain as she tried to portray to others.

"If you carry on trying to grab my hands, bitch, I'll fucking break them, and your arms, so back off," Jane yelled.

Marlene panted heavily and seemed breathless. Jane imagined she was shell-shocked that she'd actually stood up to her and taken her down without hardly having to lay a finger on her. "Okay . . . okay. I'll stop."

"You'd better because you've really pissed me off with your bad attitude, and I still haven't forgiven you for the way you spoke to me and Ethan at the wake."

"Oh, go to Hell."

"Yeah, right. I'm saving that place for you, darling, because that's where you'll be going by the time I've finished with you." Jane gripped the handcuff chain tighter with one hand and maintained her grip on Marlene's hair with her other one. Using all her strength, Jane started pulling Marlene to the side of the cage.

Marlene's screams echoed around the warehouse, and she reluctantly used her feet and legs to move in the direction Jane was taking her. "You fucking bitch! Stop pulling my fucking hair and trying to pull my arm out of its socket!"

Jane ignored her pleas and continued to pull and steer Marlene to the side of the cage. Marlene grabbed Jane's hand that was pulling her hair, and she attempted to stand up. Jane turned to her side and stamped down on Marlene's knee cap with her foot. Marlene screamed and grabbed it with her free hand.

"You vicious fucking bitch."

"Yeah. No more than you, love, but unfortunately for you, I can handle myself a bit better than you can."

Marlene swung her left arm back, and Jane swung her right leg round to her front and stomped the heel of her foot on Marlene's stomach, and she yelped.

"Oh, come on, babe. Are you really that stupid? I think I've got the upper hand here, so be a good girl and cooperate."

"Cooperate. With you? You must be joking."

"Have it your way, love. Just do me a favour and shut the fuck up and don't try anything else."

Jane continued to forcibly move Marlene to the edge of the cage, and when she started using her feet to push herself back, Jane assumed she'd finally given in to defeat and wanted to reduce the amount of pain Jane was subjecting her to.

As soon as she could, Jane put the other handcuff around two strips of the wire mesh surrounding the cage. "Right. Now I've got you where I want you, do you wanna start talking before I call the police?"

"I ain't saying nothing until my lawyer's present. You're a

scumbag cop, and I know it. I want my lawyer here."

"I already told you I don't work for the police. So, you have one of two options. You can either talk to me, or you talk to the police."

"I ain't talking to any of you because you can't prove anything. I want my lawyer, and that's that."

"Oh, right. So you're telling me you didn't come here to get Desmond's shorts back? Why didn't you come here yesterday to get them? In fact, why did you leave them here in the first place?"

Marlene glared at Jane and spat on the floor. "I ain't saying anything until my lawyer's here."

"Fine. Have it your way. Give me your lawyer's number, and I'll call them." Jane walked to her handbag and took out her mobile phone. "Right. What's their name and number?"

Marlene looked up at Jane and laughed. "You sure you wanna call him? He's gonna make mincemeat out of you."

"Oh, right. Just like you did?"

"Ha, ha, ha. Very fucking funny. You had a lucky getaway. When I'm out of these cuffs, I'm gonna beat you to a pulp and not even your own family will recognise you."

"Yeah, whatever. Less of the big talk, sweetheart, and let's give your lawyer a call."

Marlene spat toward Jane's feet again and snarled. "I fucking hate you!"

Jane laughed and shrugged her shoulders. "If it's any consolation, love, the feeling's mutual. Now can you stop being such a big mouthed pussy and give me your lawyer's name and number."

"I don't remember his fucking number. It's stored in my phone."

"And where's your phone?"

"In my handbag."

"That's fine. I'll get it. What name am I looking for?"

"Richard Heartgrove."

"Does your phone have a password?"

"Yeah. It's four-four-two-five."

"Great. I'll go and give him a call. I just hope he's available to take my call. See you in a bit."

"Tell his secretary you're calling on my behalf, and he'll drop everything to get here."

"My, my . . . I take it we have friends in high places?"

"Higher than you could dream of, you low life scum bitch."

Jane shook her head and tutted. "Now, now . . . that's not a very nice way to talk to me, and you have no idea what friends I have and what high places they sit in, so if I were you, I'd be very careful and keep that vile mouth of yours shut before it gets you into any more trouble."

Jane took Marlene's phone out of her handbag, left the ring and walked toward the exit door. Every few seconds she turned around to check Marlene hadn't broken free from her restraints. She was trying to escape, but the wire mesh was too strong for her to break it so Jane was confident Marlene would still be where she'd left her when she returned.

When she was out of the warehouse and out of Marlene's hearing range, Jane made a phone call, but she used her own phone, and she wasn't phoning Richard Heartgrove.

CHAPTER FIFTEEN

A s Jane's phone rang, she put Marlene's phone in her handbag. She impatiently tapped her foot on the ground as she waited for the call to connect.

"Hi, Jane. How's it going?" Ethan asked.

"So far, so good. I found the shorts Desmond was wearing the night of the fight and Marlene turned up about ten minutes after I'd arrived and tried to beat the crap out of me, but thankfully I managed to take her down, and now she's handcuffed to the cage."

"Gees. I hope you didn't get hurt?"

"Nah. She's all about power and strength, and isn't very good when it comes to speed and reflexes. She never got the chance to lay a finger on me."

"So, have you called the police?"

"No. Not yet. She won't talk to me, and I don't want to beat it out of her because then I'd be in trouble. But I want to find out what really happened and what she did before her bent lawyer gets involved. No doubt they'll come up with some cock and bull story to protect her and then she'll be off the hook."

"Okay. That makes sense, I suppose. You're the investigator so I'll trust your judgement and Sylvia would be livid if that happened. So what can I do to help? I don't think she'll talk to me any more than she'll talk to you."

"I agree. But I thought she might talk to Dan and Mike if they lean on her a bit and put her under pressure. Are they still there?"

"Hmm. Dan is, but Mike left about ten minutes ago."

Jane paused for a few seconds. "Okay, would you ask Dan if he'd meet me here? Tell him what's happened and I'm sure he won't have too much of a problem dragging the truth out of Marlene. I can't, but I'm sure he'd be more than happy to."

"I'm pretty sure Dan and Sylvia would be more than happy to. Leave it with me, and I'll call you back to confirm or send you a text."

"That'd be great, but talk to him as soon as you can. I've got her restrained, but I don't want to leave her on her own for too long just in case she finds a way to release herself."

"Sure. No problem. I'll go and speak to him now."

"Thanks, and I hope to hear from you soon."

Ethan disconnected the call and took a deep breath. His mind was awash with mixed emotions. If Marlene had been the person responsible for killing Christopher, then he wanted to beat the crap out of her personally, but he knew everything had to be dealt with correctly so she was convicted and nobody got into trouble. He was concerned that once he'd told Dan what Jane had just told him, he'd blow a gasket and beat her to death if he had to so he could get the truth out of her. Even if she told him the truth before he'd done that, he still feared that he'd beat her to death so that justice and revenge were served.

Feeling confused but relieved that it looked like they'd found Christopher's killer, Ethan quickly put his mobile phone in his jacket pocket and looked around to find Dan who was standing on his own in the garden, seemingly staring into space.

Ethan approached Dan hurriedly and tapped him on the shoulder. Dan shuddered and turned around. "Uff . . . sorry, Ethan. I was in a world of my own there."

"Sorry to have startled you, but I just got a phone call from Jane, and she needs our help."

Dan grabbed Ethan's forearms and gasped. "What? What is it?"

Ethan grimaced and lowered his head. "Dan. There's something I need to tell you that I should have told you, but I couldn't."

Dan shook Ethan's arms. "What? Whatever it is, you can tell me now. I don't care what it is."

"Okay, I'll tell you, but there's no time to waste, so can we talk in the car?"

"Of course, but where are we going?"

Ethan looked at Dan and exhaled. "To the warehouse."

"What the fuck? What's happening there?"

"I'll explain once we're on our way, but we have to leave now. Are you okay to drive?"

"Yeah, sure. Come on. Let's get out of here and on our way. I need to know why we're going there and what I need to prepare myself for."

"No problem, but let's just go, now!"

Ethan and Dan quickly said their goodbyes to the other mourners who were still at Sylvia's. Before leaving, Ethan pulled Patricia to one side and explained what Jane had told him and told her that he and Dan were going to the warehouse. She assured Ethan she'd let Sylvia know what was going on.

Dan was sitting in his car, and the engine was running when Ethan arrived. Dan ushered him with his hand to hurry up and get into the passenger seat. Once his door was shut, and his seatbelt was on, Dan sped away and demanded that Ethan tell him what had happened.

Ethan told Dan who Jane was, and that she was with Marlene in the warehouse. He filled him in on what had happened at the warehouse and everything that had happened on the build-up to the point.

As they drove, Ethan noticed they weren't driving toward the warehouse. "Dan, where the fuck are we going? This isn't the way to the warehouse."

Dan looked at Ethan and smirked. "I want to stop by my place on the way. I'll only be a minute, but I need to get something."

Ethan's body tensed, and he glared at Dan. "Dan, I hope you're not thinking about doing something stupid?"

Dan shrugged his shoulders and grunted. "Nothing more stupid than what that bitch, Marlene, has done."

Ethan gasped and clutched his forehead with his hand. "Jesus, Dan. This could get us all into trouble. Please think carefully about what you're going to do before you do it, for all our sakes."

Dan put a hand on Ethan's forearm and squeezed it. "Don't worry, Ethan. You and Jane will be fine. If something happens to me, then so be it. I really don't give a fuck right now. Based on what I've got planned that bitch will tell me the truth, and I won't have to lay a finger on her or pull a trigger."

Ethan pushed himself into the back of his chair and unconsciously clapped his hands in front of his face. "Well, that's a relief to hear. The last thing we need on our hands at the moment is another dead body."

Dan quickly turned to Ethan and winked. "Don't worry. Just trust me. I know exactly what I'm doing, and I've had it planned since Christopher was killed, so I've had time to think through the consequences."

"Jesus, Dan. You've just made me more nervous than I was before."

Dan gently slapped Ethan's thigh a few times and chuckled. "Hey, just chill out. I've got this all under control."

"Okay. I'll take your word for it, but please don't do anything you might regret later."

"I won't do anything I might regret. You have my word on that."

They arrived at Dan's house, and Dan told Ethan to wait in the car. Ethan remembered he hadn't called Jane, so he seized the opportunity to send her a text to let her know they were on their way and would be there in about twenty minutes. Jane responded, thanking him and reassured him that everything was under control.

Once Ethan had read Jane's message, he looked toward Dan's house and saw him shutting the front door behind him. He took a number of deep breathes through his nose and breathed out slowly through his mouth in an attempt to brace himself for what was going to happen next.

CHAPTER SIXTEEN

The hairs on Dan's forearms stood on end when he walked through the entrance to the warehouse. The last thing he'd wanted to do was revisit the place where his adopted son had been murdered. But he was on a mission, and he knew in his heart and mind he wouldn't be able to rest or draw closure on Christopher's death until he'd found out who'd killed him. He'd been making his own investigations, but thanks to Jane, he was one step closer to finding the person who he wanted to pay the price for murdering what he considered to be his beloved son.

When he saw the cage in the distance, Dan shuddered and paused. It brought back so many horrid memories, and it seemed ironic that he'd be meeting who he thought was Christopher's killer in the same cage where they'd taken Christopher's life.

Once he'd gained control of his mind and emotions, Dan started walking toward the cage, and his gaze was fixed on Jane. He could hear Ethan's footsteps behind him, and he hoped that what he was about to do was going to be in all their best interests—that justice would be served for all of them, including Sylvia.

Dan strutted toward the cage and Jane looked down at him. "Thanks for coming. Both of you."

Dan nodded and walked up the steps to the cage. "Okay. So there she is." Dan stopped when he reached Jane. "Thanks, Jane, but I'll take over from here. It won't be in your best interests to witness what's about to happen, and it could compromise your career."

Jane looked at Ethan and held her hands out to the side. "Maybe you should leave, Jane. I think your work is done for the time being. I'll give you a call if we need anything else, and I'll make sure Sylvia settles the invoice with your company."

Jane reached into her handbag and handed Marlene's mobile phone and the handcuff key to Ethan. "These might come in handy at some point. The password for the phone is four-four-two-five. Give me a call if you forget it."

Ethan took the mobile and key and nodded. "Thanks for everything, Jane. We wouldn't have got to where we are without you."

"Think nothing of it, and I hope you have the person who's responsible."

"Well, I think we're about to find out."

Jane turned around and walked to the cage door.

"Where the fuck are you going?" Marlene screamed. "You can't just walk out of here and leave me with this maniac."

Jane stopped, turned around and held her hands out to her side. "I'm sorry, Marlene, but I don't work for the police. This is a private matter for you three to sort out and my client has told me my services are no longer required, so there's nothing I can do. I'm out of here. Good luck." Jane carried on walking, went down the steps and toward the exit door.

Dan looked at Marlene, snarled and walked toward her. "That's better. Now we're on our own."

Marlene's eyes widened, and she frantically pulled against the handcuff that was attached to the cage. "Dan. You'd best back off and leave me alone. You know you'll be a dead man if you touch me."

Dan grunted and shook his head. "Now that you've murdered Christopher, I might as well be dead, so don't think that idle threats are gonna scare me."

"I swear to God, Dan, I didn't kill him."

"Well, how come Jane found the shorts Desmond wore on the night of the fight in Desmond's changing room, and you followed her here to try to take her out? Not that you managed to do a very good job of that."

Marlene panted, and her eyes bulged. "Okay . . . okay. I'll admit I sewed the syringes into Desmond's shorts, but I thought they were full of a sedative that would slow him down. I didn't think they'd kill him."

Ethan cleared his throat. "Marlene, the syringes were full of heroin, and that's what killed Christopher."

"What?" Marlene screamed. Her voice echoed around the almost empty warehouse, and once again the pigeons took to flight. "You've got to be fucking kidding me, right?"

"I wish I was, Marlene, but I went to see Christopher at the mortuary, and at Jane's request, I took a blood sample which proved positive for heroin . . . and lots of it."

Dan turned to look at Ethan. "So you've known all along then?"

"Yes, and I think you did too, Dan. The pathologist's report was obviously faked, and you told me it was the blow to his head that killed Christopher."

"I can explain. I knew the truth about how Christopher died, and I decided that until I'd got to the bottom of who'd killed him, I wouldn't tell you because I thought it would have destroyed you." Dan looked at Ethan and winced. "I did it to protect you, Ethan. I'm so sorry if I did the wrong thing."

Ethan sighed and nodded. "It's fine, Dan. I studied the video when I got home, and I knew it couldn't have been a blow to his head that killed Christopher. People don't foam at the mouth as a result of a head injury. That's why I got Jane involved."

"Oh, Jesus Christ," Marlene screamed. "What the fuck is going on? I honestly believed the blow to his head from

Desmond killed him. And can someone tell me who the hell Jane is?"

Ethan took two steps forward. "She's a private investigator, Marlene. I called her because I suspected foul play, and it didn't take long for her to work out how."

"Oh, Jesus, this is getting worse by the minute," Marlene whimpered.

"So, Marlene, you've got some explaining to do," Dan exclaimed. "Who did you get the sedative from?"

Marlene looked up at Dan and grunted. "Who do you think, Dan? Mike of course."

"Okay, so I'll be speaking to him next. And why did you want the fight rigged so Desmond would win?"

"Do you really need to ask that question?"

"Yeah, because I think there's more to it than you wanted your new boyfriend to win the fight. My suspicion is you were paid to rig the fight."

Marlene's body tensed, and she looked down at the floor. "Do you really think I'd stoop that low?"

Dan crouched down beside Marlene, put his hand under her chin and lifted her head up, so she had no choice but to look him in the eyes. "Yes, Marlene, I do think you'd stoop that low."

"Oh, come on, Dan. You know I don't need to do anything for money. If I need money, all I have to do is ask my dad, and he'll give me what I want. Happy now?"

Dan shook his head. "I'm not the least bit happy, and if you don't tell me the truth soon, then I'll get it out of you one way or the other." Without warning, Dan quickly grabbed hold of Marlene's wrist that wasn't cuffed to the cage and sat down on her thighs so she wouldn't be able to move her legs.

"What the fuck are you doing? You're hurting me! Get off me, Dan. I've got nothing more to say to you. You can do what you want because there's nothing more I can tell you."

"Oh, is that right? Well, let's find out, shall we?" Dan used his free hand to reach into his jacket pocket. He took out a filled syringe and removed the plastic protector. He waved the syringe in front of Marlene's face and laughed. "You wanna know what's in this syringe, Marlene?"

Marlene tried to pull back her arm from Dan's grip and shook her head frantically. "It had better not be what I think it is."

"It's exactly what you think it is—it's full of heroin, and if you don't tell me the truth soon, you'll be dying in the same ugly way Christopher did."

"You're fucking mad! Get that thing away from me."

Dan held Marlene's arm out in front of him and twisted it to expose her forearm. He pressed the needle against a vein and applied light pressure, but not enough to puncture the skin. "You'd better start talking, bitch, before I put the needle in."

"Ha! You wouldn't really do it. I can see through your scare tactics. You're too much of a coward to really do it."

Dan pricked the surface of the skin. "Don't fuck with me, Marlene. I'm really not in the mood."

Marlene tried to pull her arm back, so Dan gripped her wrist tighter. "Stop! You're fucking crazy," Marlene yelled.

Dan pushed the needle in a little further. "Angry and fucking mad, Marlene, so you'd better tell me what you can before I start injecting you."

"All right. Just stop will ya. I'll tell you why I did it."

"There's a good girl. Now start talking."

"I will when you take that fucking needle out of my arm."

"The needle stays in until you've told me everything you can."

Marlene looked at Dan and shook her head. "You stupid bastard. Don't you realise that once I've told you, we'll both be dead?"

"As I've already told you, I might as well be dead, and I'll take my chances. As for you, if you ever get out of prison alive, then I'd suggest you watch your back or leave the country."

Marlene huffed and blew out air. "I'm a dead woman either way."

"That you will be because if you don't tell me everything you know, then you'll be dying right here on this spot. At least you'll have some kind of chance to live if you tell me what I want to know."

"All right, all right, for Christ's sake. I was forced to do it by the big bet man."

"Okay, so this is getting interesting. And why did the big bet man force you to do it?"

"Because if Christopher had won the fight, he'd have lost shit loads of money."

"All right. I can understand that, and it wouldn't be the first time he's rigged a fight, and I'm sure it won't be the last time. The question is, do you think Mike would have supplied you with heroin as opposed to a sedative? If you don't tell me the truth, I'll pay him a visit and drag the truth out of him."

Marlene lowered her head and shook it. "I don't think it was Mike."

"Then, who was it?"

"It must have been the big bet man."

"What makes you say that?"

"Because I went to see him before the fight and took the sedative and syringes with me to show him that I'd got them. I'd already told him about my plan to sew the syringes into Desmond's shorts so he wouldn't know anything about it. I even went to the trouble of sewing a false waistband to the inside of the shorts so he wouldn't feel the plungers pressing against his body when he put the shorts on."

"And?"

"And . . . when the big bet man looked at what Mike had given me, he laughed and said it wouldn't be strong enough to slow Christopher down, so he went and got a different solution. He made me fill the syringes while I was with him, and he told me that I'd be in serious trouble if I changed them."

"Now we're getting somewhere. So the sixty-four-thousand-dollar question is . . . who's the big bet man?"

"For crying out loud, Dan, I can't betray him. He'll kill both of us."

Dan applied a little pressure to the plunger, and some of the heroin was injected into Marlene. "And why's that?"

Marlene snivelled. "Please, Dan, please don't make me do this."

"I will, and I can. Tell me . . . who's the big bet man? You've got two seconds, or the rest of this heroin is going into your bloodstream. Can you feel the effects of it already? Do you like it, Marlene?"

Marlene's face flushed red, she closed her eyes, and her head rolled backward. After a few seconds, she focused on Dan again. "Yes, I fucking can, and no, I don't like it. Jesus, Dan, you're gonna burn in Hell for this."

"And so are you if you don't hurry up and tell me."

"It's my fucking dad for crying out loud. Now take that needle out of my arm, please. I've told you what you want, so take it out, now!"

Dan carefully took the needle out of Marlene's arm, stood up, let go of her wrist and stood to one side out of punching or kicking range. "Ha! So that's where the evil bastard got all his money from, is it?"

"Yeah . . . he's got punters that deal with all the bets and payouts, and that's how he's managed to stay out of the limelight for all these years. Fuck, I can't believe I just grassed on my own flesh and blood. He's gonna kill me when he finds out I've told you."

"I wouldn't bet on it."

"Dan, what the fuck are you gonna do?"

Dan looked down at Marlene and laughed. "What do you think?"

Marlene covered her face with her hand and sobbed. "Jesus. I shouldn't have told you. You're gonna kill him, aren't you?"

Dan smirked. "I haven't made my mind up yet. I'll make that decision once I've spoken to him."

"But he might not have known it was heroin he gave me to use."

"Well, I plan to find out if he did or he didn't. And if you keep your mouth shut, we'll forget this conversation ever took place. If you don't, me or somebody else will come after you and shut you up for good. Do you get where I'm coming from?"

Marlene wiped the tears from her eyes and nodded. "So, you're not gonna call the police?"

"Not right now. If I did, it would blow the cover on the illegal fights that go on here, and then I'd have some heavy-weight mobsters coming down on me. I'd rather only have to worry about you doing something stupid rather than a few very angry bookkeepers and their heavy mob tracking me down."

"So, you're gonna let me go?"

"Once I've paid your old man a visit, I'll come back here and then I'll let you go."

"Okay. You've got a deal. I'll keep my mouth shut, but if you kill him, you know I'm gonna come after you at some point."

"I'll take my chances. And make no mistake . . . if you do come after me and manage to kill me, somebody else will come after you and kill you. Understood?"

Marlene grunted and nodded. "Understood."

Dan took his mobile phone out of his pocket. "Give me Ben's number."

"I don't remember it. Ethan's got my mobile phone, and he's listed as Dad."

Dan went to Ethan, and he handed Dan the mobile phone and told him what the password was. "I'll let you have this back when I come back. Your mum hasn't moved back in, has she? I heard Ben traded her in for a younger model some time ago, but the relationship didn't last long. Just wondered if he'd taken your mum back in or if he's on his own."

"He's on his own, thank goodness. At least my mum won't get hurt and have to witness what you might do to him."

"Pleased to hear it." Dan turned to Ethan. "I'll text you once I've done what I have to do, then I'll come back here and pick you up. Stay with her until then, and whatever you do, don't release her from that handcuff and keep a safe distance from her. Got it? Hopefully, I won't be gone too long."

"Sure. Got it."

Dan left the cage and walked toward the exit. His heart pounded harder with every step, but it wasn't because he was walking so fast, it was because his anger was mounting as he thought about the possibility of Ben deliberately changing the sedative to heroin. He was on a mission—to find Marlene's father and kill him. He'd met him a couple of times after fights and had been invited back to his house once with a group of other people to celebrate Christopher's first victory.

The biggest challenge he faced was getting Ben on his own—when he wasn't being protected by one of his security guards. He looked at the time on his phone, and given it was 19:00, he hoped Ben would be at home on his own eating dinner or watching TV.

Once he was in his car, Dan called Ben using Marlene's phone. Initially, he was surprised to hear Dan's voice say hello so Dan hurriedly explained that Marlene was in trouble with one of his rivals. He emphasised he needed to see him in private as a matter of urgency. After a momentary pause, Ben told Dan to get to his place as soon as possible so he could tell him what trouble Marlene was in. Dan sensed an element of concern and frustration in Ben's voice, and that pleased him.

CHAPTER SEVENTEEN

Dan pulled up outside Ben's impressive detached two-storey house that was surrounded by high perimeter walls that were only broken by a spiked metal barred electric gate that allowed cars to enter and leave. Beside it was a smaller gate that allowed people to enter and leave if they weren't driving or welcome to park in Ben's double fronted garage that was separate from the main house.

Dan parked in the street between Ben's house and his neighbour's house. He looked at the clock on the dashboard. It was 19:20, and the evening light was fading. He got out of his car, locked it and walked toward the front gate. He stood in front of the video entry screen and pressed the intercom buzzer. A few seconds later, it connected.

"Hi, Dan. Are you on your own?"

"Yeah, I'm on my own."

There was a buzzing sound, and Dan pushed the gate open. He walked along the path to the front door and stood in front of the spy hole. After a couple of seconds, the door opened slightly, and Ben's round, bloated face appeared through the gap. The door opened wider, but Ben kept behind the door.

"Come in, Dan."

Dan walked through the front door into the hallway, and he heard the door quickly close behind him. Ben's short and rotund frame waddled in front of him and led them along the hallway toward the back of the house.

Dan despised Ben for what he'd done to Christopher, and

that he'd overindulged in life's luxuries as a consequence of treading on and threatening whoever tried to get in the way of him preserving and growing the fortune he'd accumulated over the years.

"I thought we'd go through to the conservatory," Ben said hastily.

"That's fine. I don't mind where we talk, but we need to talk fast. Marlene's life is in danger, and you need to make some tough decisions."

"For crying out loud, what's the stupid cow got herself into now?"

"Well, she's in safe hands at the moment, but that could all change at the drop of a hat."

"For fuck sake. Why does trouble always follow that girl of mine? She brings it on herself half the time, I know, but she's my daughter, so I've gotta look after her, ain't I?"

"That you do, Ben. That you do."

They walked into the conservatory and Ben indicated for Dan to take a seat. Ben walked toward a drinks trolley and looked at Dan. "I think I might need a drink. You want one?"

Dan raised a hand. "I'm fine, Ben. I'm driving, so I'd better not."

"Suit yourself." Ben poured himself a glass of what looked like scotch and sat down on a chair in front of Dan. "So what kinda trouble is she in? And who's she in trouble with?"

"I'll come onto that, but first I need to ask you a few questions. You might be able to sort this mess out just by answering the questions."

Ben looked at Dan quizzically. "I don't get ya. What the fuck you talking about?"

"Well, I've spoken to Marlene, and she admitted to doping Christopher on the night of the fight. You know . . . sewing syringes into Desmond's shorts?"

"Course, I know. She told me what she was gonna do.

And? What the fuck has that got to do with anything?"

"I think you know the answer to that question, Ben."

"Nah, I don't actually. So please, explain to me why you've really come here."

"Because Marlene told me you gave her a different solution to fill the syringes with."

"Why, the fucking little bitch. So she grassed on me? Me own fucking daughter grassed on me?" Ben sat back in his chair and took a sip of his drink. He looked at Dan. "Okay. So I might have. So what?"

"So, the liquid you gave her to fill the syringes with was heroin. Did you know it was heroin?"

"How the fuck do you know that? And how can you prove it?"

"That's irrelevant at the moment, but rest assured, I've got enough evidence to put you and Marlene behind bars for the rest of your sad, miserable lives."

Ben stood up and pointed at Dan. "I'm telling you now, wise guy, if you breathe one word of this to the police, you're a dead man. Even if I am in the nick, I've got plenty of people on the outside who'll come after you and kill ya, so I think you'd better leave now, and we'll pretend this conversation never took place. Understood?"

"I'm afraid it's not that easy for me, Ben."

"What ya talking about? Go away, silly man, and stop wasting my time."

"I'm afraid I can't do that, Ben. You killed Christopher, and he was like a son to me, so now you're gonna have to pay the price for what you've done."

Ben held his hands out to his side. "So what ya gonna do, brave man? Shoot me in cold blood?"

Dan stood up and shook his head. He reached into his jacket pocket, and before he had a chance to take the syringe out, Ben threw his glass at him and started running toward a unit behind him.

Even though the glass had caught Dan on his shoulder and the pain was intense, he ignored it and chased after Ben. When he was close enough, Dan rugby-tackled Ben down to the ground and placed all his weight on top of him.

Ben lashed out with his hands and tried to hit Dan on his head and face. "Get the fuck off me, you bastard. Tell me what you want. I'll give you anything. Just don't kill me."

"Too late for negotiations now, Ben." Dan reached into his jacket pocket and grabbed the syringe. Once the protective cap was off, he stabbed the needle into a bulging vein in Ben's neck and pushed the plunger until the syringe was empty.

After a few seconds, Ben stopped trying to fight Dan off. Dan raised himself using his hands and legs. He looked down at Ben, and his head was tilted to the right. He looked at his eyes, and his pupils were dilated. After a few seconds, his body went into spasms, and his breathing became shallower. Ben's body made its last attempt to get the drug out of it, and he spewed vomit all over the floor. His lips started turning a bluish colour, and a few seconds later, Ben feebly reached a hand out to his throat, but it slumped on the floor before it got there.

Dan crouched down beside Ben, and he couldn't hear or see any signs of him breathing. Satisfied his job was done, Dan pulled the syringe out of Ben's neck, replaced the protective cap and put it in his jacket pocket.

Conscious there were CCTV cameras all around the house, Dan went in search of the monitoring and recording equipment. He went to the place where he thought it would most likely be—Ben's office. Besides the large monitor, keyboard and mouse on top of an oak desk was a smaller monitor which displayed images of what the CCTV cameras were recording. Dan disconnected the hard drive, picked it up and left the office with it tucked under his left arm.

Dan walked to the front door, took a handkerchief out of his jacket pocket, opened the door and closed it behind him, being careful not to leave any fingerprints behind. With his handkerchief covering his fingers, he pressed the exit button on the garden gate, opened it and left Ben's house. He got into his car and started to drive toward the warehouse.

As he drove, Dan reflected on any traces he might have left at Ben's place to demonstrate that he'd been there. He'd taken the hard drive for the CCTV recording equipment, so there was no footage of him being at the house, and apart from fibres from his clothes, he couldn't think of anything else. He hadn't touched Ben with his hands. Only his clothed body had touched him, so he was reasonably confident that if he disposed of all his clothes and fully valeted his car, the police would have a hard time trying to prove it was him who'd killed Ben. He'd called Ben from Marlene's phone, so the call couldn't be traced to him.

Dan's continued freedom all depended on whether Marlene kept her mouth shut or not. He had no idea how she'd react when she found out her dad was dead, but she had as much to lose as Dan if the police found out what had really happened so he hoped she'd keep her mouth shut.

CHAPTER EIGHTEEN

It was dark when Dan arrived at the warehouse, and he imagined Ethan had been cursing him for leaving him there so long in the dark with Marlene. He grabbed his flashlight from the toolbox in his car and entered the warehouse. When he entered the main warehouse, Ethan called out to ask if it was him and he reassured him it was. As he approached the cage, he could see Marlene's head slumped forward, and Dan imagined the heroin had made her drowsy, so he suspected she'd been out for the count for some time.

Dan stepped into the cage and walked toward Ethan. "Has she been asleep for long?"

"After an initial rant and some water, she passed out. I don't know how much heroin you gave her, but she was off her nut for a while. Pretty scary to look at, actually."

"Yeah, well, she deserved it. Anyway, let's just say the rest of the heroin has been put to good use."

"You mean—"

"Ethan, the less you know, the better. I don't want you to be incriminated in any way, but suffice to say justice has been served."

"But, Dan. Aren't you worried the police will catch up with you, and you'll be sent to prison?"

"I think I've covered my tracks pretty well, but there's some things I need to do urgently so let's get the hell out of here so I can take you to Sylvia's and I can get on with what I need to do."

Ethan turned toward Marlene. "And what about her? What

are we going to do with her?"

"Just leave the key to the handcuffs by her side, and she can release herself when she wakes up. I take it she's still breathing?"

"Yeah, she's been making weird noises and talking gibberish, every now and again, so she's still very much alive."

"Okay, that's good. Right, go and leave the key and let's get out of here."

Ethan walked over to Marlene and placed the key by her hand. Dan followed him and placed his flashlight by her side, so the light was pointing toward the exit door. "She might need this when she wakes up. You never know, she might be scared of the dark."

Ethan chuckled. "You're a big softy at heart."

"She won't think that when she goes to visit her old man."

"Okay. Come on. Let's get out of here. Sylvia will be wondering what the hell's happened to us both."

"Well, I'm sure she'll be more than happy when you tell her that justice has been served. And in a way that I'm sure she'd find very fitting." Dan wiped Marlene's phone with his handkerchief and put it back in her handbag.

Dan and Ethan left the warehouse, and Dan drove Ethan to Sylvia's house. When he saw the door open, Dan pulled away and started to drive. He wanted to get out of his clothes, have a shower, then hoover his car seats and clean the inside and outside of it thoroughly as soon as he could.

When Ethan walked through the door, Sylvia shut it behind him, then gave him a hug. "So tell me. What happened? Was it Marlene?"

Ethan turned to Sylvia and winced. "In some ways, yes, but in other ways no."

"Okay, well, that doesn't make much sense. Come on, let's

go through to the sitting room and you can tell me and Patricia everything you know. Do you want a drink?"

"Yes, please. The stronger, the better. I need it after today."

"Of course you do, my darling. Come on. Let's go and get you a nice drink to help you relax a little."

When they entered the sitting room, Patricia greeted Ethan and Sylvia went to the drinks cabinet. What do you want to drink, Ethan?"

"I'll have a large neat scotch, please."

"Oh dear, it sounds like you've had a trying day," Patricia commented.

Ethan looked at Patricia and nodded. "A very trying day, but also a very eventful day."

Sylvia walked toward Ethan and handed him his drink. She took a seat beside Patricia on the sofa opposite him and sat back. "So, explain to us why Marlene did have something to do with Christopher's death, but then again, she didn't."

Ethan recounted what Marlene had told him and Dan at the warehouse and that Dan had gone to see Ben. When he returned, he'd simply told Ethan the rest of the heroin had been put to good use and that justice had been served.

Sylvia and Patricia both gasped. Sylvia clapped her hands together and smiled. "Did Dan tell you he'd injected Ben with the heroin?"

Ethan shook his head and took a sip of his drink. "Not exactly, but it's pretty obvious he did."

"What a brave and valiant man, and it just goes to show how much Christopher meant to him. If I'm perfectly honest, I want to give Dan a hug and thank him personally for making sure the appropriate justice was served. I couldn't have thought of a better way to kill Christopher's murderer. He's given him a bit of his own medicine, so to speak."

"That he certainly has, Sylvia. My only concern is that Marlene will go to the police or hire somebody to kill Dan."

"Yes. I'm sure once she discovers that Dan's killed her father, she might decide to take revenge, but I'm sure Dan's big enough and wise enough to look after himself. And if she does go after him, I'll hire a hit man to go after her, and I'll tell her that to her face. She's the one who instigated the doping, and Ben took it to another level, so I wouldn't have any problem whatsoever finding somebody to scare her off or kill her. Dan has done everything I wish I could have done for Christopher, so I feel it's my personal duty to make sure he's looked after."

"Well, Marlene has a lot at stake if she does try and go after Dan. He's already threatened her that if she goes after him or someone does manage to kill him, then somebody will go after her."

"Well, if the stupid woman has any sense, she'll leave Dan alone and get on with her life without her father. I can't imagine she'll be half as brave or cocky, knowing her father isn't around to protect her."

"I certainly hope you're right."

"Right, now that we've got that out of the way. Are you hungry? You must be starved."

"I must admit, I'm a little peckish. It's been a long day, and I haven't eaten anything all day, so a little snack or something would be nice."

"Nonsense, darling. Patricia has made a nice lasagna that we can have with some salad. We were just about to eat before you arrived, so you've timed it perfectly."

"That'd be great. I'm sure I'll be able to manage a small portion of lasagna and some salad."

"Excellent. Shall we go through to the kitchen, then?"

"Sure. I'll just finish my drink, and then, I'm ready." Ethan drained his glass and put the empty glass on a coaster on the coffee table in front of him.

The three of them went through to the kitchen and Sylvia opened a bottle of red wine, and Patricia went to the oven and took the lasagna out. She took it to the table and placed it on a wooden board in the middle of the table and went to the fridge to get the salad.

While they ate, they spoke about how the day had gone, and Sylvia suggested that Ethan invited Dan to dinner at her house one evening so she could thank him in person for what he'd done. She also stated she wanted to hold a small intimate service for Christopher with just the four of them so they could all pay their final respects to him. Ethan and Patricia agreed it would be a nice gesture if Dan was invited, and that it should just be the four of them who attended.

CHAPTER NINETEEN

Marlene woke up. Her head was groggy, and her neck ached. She looked up, and all she could see was a bright light in front of her. She shook her head, and her first thought was that she was in Heaven. Was that what Heaven looked like? Was she about to meet God? She quickly turned to her left and saw the wire mesh of the cage and breathed a sigh of relief. She was still alive and still in the cage.

Once she'd come to her senses, she realised her wrist was still handcuffed to the cage. She looked either side of her to see if she could see Dan or Ethan, but there was no sign of them.

When she realised that she was there on her own, she called out for help, but nobody responded. The palms of her hands started sweating, and her heartbeat increased. Had Dan and Ethan left her there to die? Why weren't they there?

Marlene felt dizzy, and her head spun at the thought of being left there to die of dehydration or starvation. She closed her eyes and put her free hand down on the floor to try and stabilise herself. She felt something she was sure was a small metal key pressed against the palm of her hand. She opened her eyes, moved her hand to the side and saw the small key which she assumed was the key to unlock the handcuffs.

Marlene looked up to the sky and crossed herself. At least Dan and Ethan hadn't left her there to rot to death. Her hand trembled as she picked the key up between her thumb and index finger. If it slipped out of her fingers and dropped out of the cage as she tried to unlock the handcuff, she was doomed.

Once she had a stable grip on it, she looked up at the hand-cuff and raised her hand. She used her forefinger to feel around the handcuff to find the keyhole. Once she'd located it, she slipped the key in and turned it. The handcuff released and she supported her arm with her other hand because it had gone to sleep after being in a raised position for so long.

Once the blood had flowed back into her arm and the pins and needles had passed, her mind sprang into action. Had her dad managed to calm Dan down and convince him it wasn't him or that it wasn't his intention to kill Christopher? Or had Dan killed him?

Marlene tentatively stood up and stayed where she was for a few seconds while her body came back to life. Once she was confident that she wasn't going to collapse or pass out, she slowly walked toward her handbag and fumbled through it to see if her mobile phone was in it.

She breathed a sigh of relief when she felt the familiar rec-tangular device touch her fingers and quickly took it out of her handbag. She checked her call log and saw that Dan must have called Ben using her phone at three minutes past seven. She hit the call button and waited anxiously for her dad to answer. When the phone just kept ringing, her heart pounded, and her hand started trembling. When the phone went through to voicemail, she ended the call and put her phone back in her handbag.

She put her handbag on her shoulder, grabbed the flash-light and used it to guide her out of what she now considered to be a Hell hole.

She drove as fast but as safely as she could to her dad's house. The last thing she wanted to do was exceed the speed limit and get stopped by the police. For all she knew, Dan might have already reported her to the police, so if she had been stopped, there was a possibility she'd have been arrested and taken into custody immediately.

When she arrived at her dad's house, Marlene fumbled around in her handbag for her key chain that had a copy of her father's house keys on it. She opened the security gate, ran along the pathway, let herself into the house and closed the door behind her. "Dad. Dad. Are you here?"

There was no response, so Marlene ran into the sitting room, but there was no sign of her dad. She left and ran down the hallway toward the kitchen and conservatory. "Dad. Dad. Where are you?"

There was still no response. Marlene checked the kitchen, but there was no sign of her dad. She left and ran to the conservatory. She stopped in her tracks when she saw her dad lying on the floor motionless.

Marlene ran over to him, knelt down beside him and yelped when she looked down at his face because it appeared to be as solid as dry clay. His open eyes and mouth portrayed a look of shock and horror, and she imagined he must have been petrified before he'd taken his last breath.

She quickly checked his wrist for a pulse, but there was nothing. She pressed her forefinger and index finger against his neck. It was rigid, and there was no sign of a pulse. She covered her mouth with her hands and sobbed. "You bastard, Dan. I can't believe you've actually killed my dad."

After she'd cried for a few minutes and done her best to come to terms with the fact that her dad was dead, Marlene stroked his head and cuddled his still body.

Realising there was nothing she could do to help her dad or bring him back to life, Marlene's thoughts turned to herself and her future. Should she go to the police and grass on Dan or should she just accept that she'd be starting a life long battle with him if she did?

Marlene stood up and sat down on the armchair where she

figured Dan had sat. She stared at her dead father's body, covered her mouth with her hands and took a deep breath. What was the best thing to do? Her dad was dead, so he wasn't going to be around to protect her in the future.

After carefully considering her options, Marlene decided it was best, in the short term, to make Dan think he'd won the battle. Once she'd got over the shock of losing her dad and was thinking more rationally, then she'd decide how to deal with Dan, if she decided to deal with him at all. She was in a catch twenty-two, and for the time being, she had to put her own safety and interests at heart.

After seeing the way Christopher had died, Marlene knew her dad had been killed by a heroin overdose, so she started to plan what to do next. She decided she'd stage it to look as if a desperate junkie had broken into her dad's house. When he'd approached him, they'd got into a fight, and the junkie had stabbed her dad in the neck with a needle that was full of some kind of drug.

Convinced her plan would work, Marlene went to the kitchen and searched through the cupboard under the sink for a pair of rubber gloves and a plastic bag. When she found them, she went upstairs and ransacked the bedrooms — pulled all the drawers open, threw paintings that were hung on the wall on the floor and tossed clothes all over the place — to make it look like somebody had rummaged through everything to try and find money and jewellery.

The only way a robber could have broken into the house would have been by scaling the high perimeter walls or following her dad in when he drove through the open electric gate. So Marlene wanted to make it look as if the burglar had only been interested in small items of value that they'd be able to escape with easily.

To make it look more convincing, Marlene stuffed her dad's watches and jewellery into the plastic bag. She knew it was all insured, so her dad's insurance company would be able to validate that it was missing.

Once she'd finished ransacking the upstairs bedrooms, Marlene went downstairs into the study and the sitting room. She emptied the contents of drawers, cupboards and anything else she could see where a robber might have thought money or valuables had been hidden.

When she went into her dad's office, she noticed the hard drive connected to the CCTV monitoring system had been taken, and she cursed Dan for having done such a thorough job of covering his tracks. She ransacked the office and then took the plastic bag with her dad's jewellery in it out to her car, hid it in the glove compartment and locked it.

Marlene went back into the house and sat down so she could collect her thoughts before she called the police. She wanted to make sure she'd covered everything to make it look as if the house had been burgled and her dad had surprised them. She went back to the conservatory and opened the sliding doors. Once she'd done that, she went to the kitchen, opened the unit under the sink, took the rubber gloves off and put them back where she'd found them.

Once she'd got her plan as clear as she could in her head, she looked at her phone and saw it was 21:35. She dialled nine-nine-nine and waited for the call to connect.

"Hello, you're through to emergency services. How can I help you?"

Marlene snivelled and coughed. "Hi, I need you to send somebody to my father's house as soon as possible. I've just arrived, and he's lying dead on the floor in the conservatory. By the looks of it, somebody's broken in and injected him in the neck with something. There's vomit by his side, and his lips are kind of a bluish colour. Can you please send somebody immediately? I'm scared that whoever did it might still be in the house or come back. The conservatory doors are wide open, but I don't want to touch them just in case I need to make a quick escape."

"Okay, madam. Are you sure he's dead? Have you checked for a pulse?

"Yes, I have, and he hasn't got one."

"Okay, madam, that may be so, but I'll arrange for a paramedic team to be sent to the house. They might still be able to resuscitate him. Can you please let me have your name and the address, and I'll make that my first priority."

Marlene told the operator her full name and the address.

"Thank you, madam. I'm just going to put you on hold for a minute so I can make arrangements for the paramedic team to get to you as soon as possible. Please stay on the line. I'll be right back."

"Okay, but please hurry. Whoever did it could still be in the house."

"I will, madam."

After a momentary silence, the call connected again.

"Okay, madam, the paramedic team are on their way. Do you have any reason to believe somebody may be in the house with you? Has anybody tried to attack you? Have you heard anybody?"

"Well, nobody tried to attack me when I walked through the door, and nobody has up until now, and I haven't heard anybody, but they could be hiding upstairs, and I'm too scared to go up there and look. All the rooms downstairs look as if they've been absolutely ransacked, so somebody was clearly looking for something. I don't know what to do for the best. I'm too scared to leave the house just in case they're outside, and I'm too scared to stay inside it. If whoever killed my dad is still in the house, then I don't want to shut the conservatory doors, but if they're outside in the garden, then I do. How long will it take for somebody to get here? I need somebody here as soon as possible before something happens to me."

"Okay, madam. Are you in the conservatory now?"

"Yes."

"Okay. It'd be better if you don't touch the doors because you might interfere with vital clues and evidence. Is there anywhere you can wait where you can see if anybody approaches you from the garden or inside the house?"

Marlene paused to think. "Yes. If I stand in the doorway of the conservatory, I can see the open doors and the hallway that leads to the conservatory."

"Okay. Wait there, and if anybody approaches you from the garden, I'm assuming you can escape through the front door?"

"I can, but if there's more than one of them and they approach me from different angles, then I'm gonna be in serious trouble."

"I understand, madam, I'm requesting urgent police assistance as we speak so somebody will be with you very soon. Please keep your phone by you and whoever I send to the house will call you to let you know it's the ambulance or police arriving so you can let them in."

"Okay. But how long will it take for someone to get here?"

"I'll get them there as soon as I can."

"Okay. The sooner, the better. I'm standing in the doorway of the conservatory, and I'll keep my eyes on the conservatory doors and hallway."

"Okay, madam, that's very sensible. Somebody will be with you very shortly, so try to stay calm."

"I'll do my best, and thank you."

"No problem. It's my job, madam."

"Okay, somebody else is trying to call me, so I'm going to hang up because it's probably the paramedics or the police."

"Okay, madam. Goodnight."

Marlene accepted the other incoming call. "Hello, madam,

we're the paramedic team, and we're outside the front gate."

"Okay, give me a few seconds, and I'll open the gate." Marlene ran to the front door and looked at the video intercom system. She could see two male paramedics dressed in high visibility yellow jackets with grey stripes, holding what she assumed were their emergency bags, so she buzzed them in and opened the front door.

As soon as they entered the house, the taller man with a goatee beard looked down at Marlene. "Can you show us where your father is, please?"

Marlene closed the front door and ran along the hallway. She could hear the footsteps of the paramedics behind her. When she got to the end of the hallway, she turned right and ran toward the conservatory. Once she was inside, she turned to the paramedics at her side and pointed at her dad. "He's there. Please, do what you can, but I think it might be too late? I have no idea how long he's been dead. I spoke to him at seven, but he didn't answer his phone when I called him just after nine."

"We'll do what we can, madam." The paramedics ran toward Ben and crouched down beside him. As soon as they looked at him, the paramedics looked at each other and shook their heads.

The taller paramedic turned to Marlene and winced. "I'm afraid rigour mortis has already started to set in so he must have been dead for at least two hours."

"How can you tell?"

"When rigour mortis starts to set in, it affects the eyelids, neck and jaw first, then it'll affect the rest of his body. It's very clear to us that he's dead so I'm afraid there's nothing we can do for him. If you'd have found him earlier, then we might have stood a chance of saving him, but there's nothing that can be done for him now."

Marlene opened her mouth to say something, and her

phone rang. She looked at the two paramedics. "That's probably the police, so I'd better answer it."

"That's fine. Go ahead."

"Okay, I'll be back with you soon." Marlene accepted the call.

"Hello, Marlene, this is Police Constable Tracy Clarke, and I'm outside with Police Constable Michael Stuart. Are you okay?"

"Hi. I'm okay. The paramedics are here, so I'm not on my own. I'm still very shaken up, but I'm fine. Give me a few seconds, and I'll open the front gate and let you in."

"Okay, but don't hang up. Stay on the phone, all right?"

"Sure, I'm making my way to the front door now. I can't hear anybody moving, so hopefully, you've arrived in good time."

"Excellent. Keep your eyes on doors as you move and listen out for any sudden movement. We'll be with you in a matter of seconds."

"Okay, I'm going to buzz you in now." Marlene pressed the button on the intercom system, and she heard the gate buzzing.

WPC Tracy was panting. "Okay, we're through the front gate and running toward the front door."

"Okay. I'm going to open the front door."

"That's great. You'll be safe now, so try to relax."

As they approached the front door, Marlene greeted them and indicated they should enter. She closed the door behind them and looked at them both. "So what do you want to do first? The paramedics have confirmed he's dead and rigour mortis has already started to set in so do you want to check the house first to see if anybody else is in it? Nobody has approached us or tried to attack us, but I'd feel a lot more at ease if I knew there was nobody else in here with us."

WPC Tracy looked at PC Michael. "Do you want to check

the upstairs rooms, and I'll check the rooms down here?"

"Yeah, sure. Then we'll look at the body and talk to the paramedics." PC Michael took a metal baton out of its holder that was attached to his belt and extended it.

Marlene pointed along the hallway. "The stairs are on the right about halfway down the hallway." PC Michael nodded, walked toward the stairs and disappeared out of sight.

WPC Tracy looked at Marlene. "Right. You stay here while I check the rooms down here."

"Okay. Whatever you say."

WPC Tracy took her baton out of its holder, extended it and went into the sitting room. When she came out, she looked at Marlene and shrugged her shoulders. "There's nobody in there so I'll move on." She walked across the hallway and went into the study. After a minute, she came out and shook her head. "There's nobody in there either, but whoever was or is in here did a good job of ransacking the place, that's for sure. Looks like they were looking for something very specific or possibly just valuables. Have you noticed anything missing?"

"I can't say I've looked properly yet, but I did notice that whoever it was took the hard drive connected to the CCTV that recorded all the footage."

WPC Tracy frowned and scratched her chin. "Hmm. That's interesting. If it was a junkie who broke in here, they couldn't have been that high and must be pretty smart because they must have noticed all the CCTV cameras around the house and took the time to find the hard drive. Where was it?"

"In my dad's office, which is the next door along from you."

"Okay, I'll go and have a look." WPC Tracy disappeared into Ben's office, and when she was obviously satisfied there was nobody in the room, she came out and looked at Marlene. "Do you know if your father also had the CCTV system connected to an off-site server or backed-up to a cloud?"

"I'm sorry, I don't know. But knowing my father, it's highly unlikely." Marlene cleared her throat. "How can I put this . . . he was an old-fashioned and private man so I can't imagine he'd have wanted anything stored away from this house so other people could go through it."

"Hmm. That's a shame. That would have really helped us out. Perhaps later you can let me have the details of the security company who installed the system, and we can talk to them. Right, so does that just leave the kitchen and conservatory or are there any other rooms?"

"Just the kitchen and conservatory. I'll show you where the kitchen is first."

"Thanks. Just steer me in the right direction and stay behind me." When they reached the kitchen, WPC Tracy walked in, and Marlene stood in the doorway. WPC Tracy checked in the broom cupboard and the pantry, but she didn't find anybody. "Okay, well, it's all clear in here, so shall we move onto the conservatory?"

"Sure." Marlene stepped back, and when WPC Tracy passed through the doorway, Marlene pointed in front of her. "Go straight along the hallway, and the entrance to the conservatory is on the left-hand side."

WPC Tracy led the way, and once she was in the conservatory, she nodded to acknowledge the paramedics. "Marlene tells me you've pronounced him dead. Any idea of how he died and when?"

The taller paramedic cleared his throat. "Well, rigour mortis has already affected his eyelids, neck and chin, so I'd guess he died just over two hours ago. Looking at the puncture mark in his neck, together with the vomit and bluish lips, I suspect he was injected with some kind of opioid."

WPC Tracy nodded, took a pair of rubber gloves out of her pocket, put them on and walked over to Ben's body. She studied his neck, face and the vomit, then looked up at the paramedics. "Yeah, it definitely looks like your suspicion could be right."

"Okay, well given there's nothing more we can do here, we'll be on our way so we can attend the next call-out. We'll notify our control centre of our findings when we get to the ambulance, and our report will be filed as soon as possible so you'll be able to look at that fairly soon if you need to."

"Yeah, sure. Thanks."

Marlene looked at the paramedics. "Do you want me to see you to the door?"

"No, that's fine. We can find our own way out."

"Okay. There's a button in the small black box at the side of the gate. Just press it, and the gate will open."

"That's great, thanks."

The two paramedics left the conservatory. WPC Tracy turned to Marlene. "I hate to ask you this, but was your father a drug user?"

"No, he wasn't," Marlene snapped. "In fact, he was very anti-drugs and told me when I was growing up that he'd have been mortified if he ever found out that I'd taken them."

"Okay. As I said, I'm sorry I asked you that question, but we need to know as much as we can. What I don't get is why a drug addict would come here with a syringe full of what-ever was in it. Normally once a drug addict has got a fix, they tend to use it straight away."

Marlene grimaced and held her hands out to the side. "Who knows . . . maybe they had their next fix but wanted to get some money for the fix after that."

"That's true, but it'd be pretty abnormal behaviour for a junkie."

The tension in Marlene's body subsided a bit when she heard PC Michael walk into the conservatory. She hoped he would change the direction of the conversation so she didn't have to come up with any other answers to allay WPC Tracy's doubts that would blow a hole in her self-created story.

PC Michael stood beside Marlene and WPC Tracy. "Well, there's nobody upstairs, but whoever was in here was definitely looking for something. Everything's been pulled out of drawers and paintings have been thrown on the floor, so that makes me suspect they were looking for a safe and valuables."

"Yeah, I just said the same thing to Marlene. They've done the same in all the rooms down here. What I'm trying to work out is how they got in here. I mean, the security here is pretty tight, and I can't imagine anybody being able to scale the perimeter walls without some help."

"Maybe there were two of them," PC Michael suggested.

"Yeah, maybe, but I think even two people would struggle to get in here."

Marlene cleared her throat. "I think the most probable way is that they followed my dad in when he opened the electric gate to the driveway. It takes a while for the gate to close so they could have easily snuck in before it shut and laid low for a while before they entered the house through the conservatory doors."

WPC Tracy and PC Michaels nodded. "Yeah, that'd be the easiest way for sure," WPC Tracy acknowledged. "And they'd have been able to get out through the front door and gate."

"Exactly," Marlene stated.

"Well, until we get the forensic team in here, I guess we'll have to assume for the time being that whoever it was followed your father in when he drove through the gate, entered the house through the conservatory doors, and left through the front door and gate."

"Have you touched anything, Marlene?" PC Michael asked.

Marlene looked at her father. "No. Well, apart from my dad. When I saw him on the floor, the first thing I did was check to see if he had a pulse in his wrist and neck. Then when I realised he was dead, I stroked his head and cuddled him."

WPC Tracy winced. "Okay, I'll let the forensic team know. Michael, would you mind checking the back and front gardens? Given they had an easy escape route through the front, I can't imagine they'd have hung around, but just to be on the safe side."

"Sure, that's not a problem. I'll go and have a look around." PC Michael walked through the conservatory doors and into the garden.

WPC Tracy looked at Marlene. "Do you remember if you touched anything other than your father?"

Marlene shook her head gently. "No. I didn't touch anything else."

"Okay. That's great. At some point, we'll need to take your fingerprints, so we know they belong to you. I imagine your fingerprints are all over the place given it's your father's house, but it's just so we can distinguish yours from any others we find. You might also be required to provide a DNA sample and have some skin swabs taken. If you let me have all your contact details, I'll let you know where you can go to get those things done. I also need a contact number just in case we have any further questions. I'm afraid I'm going to have to ask you to leave your mobile phone with us so we can check times of calls, etcetera. A landline will be fine, but if you can let me have another mobile phone number that would be better." WPC Tracy took a small black leather notepad holder out of her top jacket pocket and held it out to Marlene. "There's a pen inside."

"Sure. That's not a problem. You tell me when and where I need to go, and I'll be there." Marlene opened the notepad holder and took the pen out. "I'll write down our landline number and my boyfriend's mobile number. His name's Desmond, but I'll write that down. I'll also write down the password for my mobile."

"Okay, so it's password protected. Presumably, you're the only person who knows the number?"

Marlene nodded. "Yep. Nobody else knows it, so I'm the only one who can use it."

"That's great. Right, while you're doing that, I'm going to call my boss so he can arrange for the forensic team to be sent here as soon as possible. They'll want to gather as much evidence as they can over the next few days, and that'll involve taking a lot of samples, prints, etcetera. Unless there's anything else you can tell us, then please feel free to go home. I'm assuming you don't live here?

"No. I live with my boyfriend, but I came to visit my dad at least once a week to see how he was and spend some time with him."

"So did he know you were coming here tonight?"

Marlene thought back to the call Dan had made to Ben when he'd left the warehouse. "Yes, I called him a few minutes after seven to check he was going to be at home this evening. When he said he would be, I told him I'd get here once me and my boyfriend had finished dinner. I called him again just after nine to let him know I was leaving home and would be with him in about half an hour, but he didn't answer the call. I assumed he was in the bathroom or something and couldn't get to his phone or was talking to somebody on the landline." Marlene shook her head and sighed. "But now I know why he didn't answer his phone."

"Okay, so if he answered his phone at just after seven and spoke to you, but didn't answer at nine, the incident must have taken place during those two hours. Probably just after seven given the paramedics have confirmed that rigour mortis has started to set in. That helps narrow things down a bit.

When the forensic team get here, PC Michael and I will go and have a chat with the neighbours to see if they saw anybody loitering around outside."

"Well, you know what's best to do, and I hope you find the person who did that to my dad."

"We'll do our very best, Marlene, but if it was a junkie, they could be pretty hard to find. Unfortunately, in this day and age, there are far too many junkies on the street, and most of them don't have a home and stray from one place to another. But rest assured we'll do whatever we can to find them and we'll be in touch with you once the forensic pathologist has determined the cause of death. And of course, once they've finished all their tests, we'll let you know when your father's body can be released so you can organise the funeral."

"Thank you. I appreciate that. And I hope whoever did it burns in Hell for what they've done."

"Okay, well if there's nothing more you can tell us now, then feel free to leave, but before you go can you let me have your mobile phone and the house keys, please? Given the forensic team will be here for a few days, they'll need to be able to let themselves in."

"That's fine but can I phone my boyfriend and mother before I give my phone to you. I want to go and see my mum, so I can tell her in person that her ex-husband is dead, and I want to let my boyfriend know that I'll be home later than planned. Otherwise, he'll worry."

"That's fine. Do you want me to leave the room?"

"It's okay. I'll go into the sitting room. I don't want to be looking at my dad's dead body when I call my mum. It'll just upset me, and I need to be strong for her sake. She's going to be heartbroken when she finds out, so I want to be with her to comfort her when I break the news to her."

"Okay. I'll see you back here once you've made the calls."

Marlene left the conservatory and walked to the sitting

room. She called Desmond first. After a few rings, he answered. "Hi, darling, it's me. I'm so sorry to leave you on your own for so long, but something tragic has happened to my dad."

"What's happened, babe? Is he all right?"

Marlene sniffled. "No, he's not all right. He's dead."

"What? You're kidding me, right?"

"I wish I was, but I'm at his house now, and the paramedics have confirmed that he's dead and rigour mortis has set in, so there was nothing they could do for him."

"Oh shit. Do you have any idea of who killed him?"

"No. I won't know anything until the forensic team have done what they need to do, and the police conduct their investigation. Anyway, look. I need to call my mum, and when I leave here, I'm going to her place so I can tell her in person what's happened."

"Do you want me to meet you there?"

"No. It's fine. I think she'll be devastated, so I'll probably spend the night there, and I don't want you leaving the house in the state of mind you're in. Will you be okay on your own?"

"Yeah. I'll be fine. Don't worry about me. Go and see your mother and give me a call later to let me know how you both are."

"Okay, darling. I will do. Gotta go now, but I'll speak to you later."

"All right, honey. A big hug and kiss for both you and your mum. My thoughts are with you."

"Thanks, darling. I'll speak to you later."

Marlene ended the call, searched through her contact list for her mum's number and hit the call button. Her hand trembled while she waited for her to answer. "Mum. It's me."

"Are you okay, sweetie? You sound a bit shaken up."

"Mum, I have to come and see you now. I've got some devastating news to break to you, but I want to tell you in person, and not on the phone."

"What is it? Please tell me what's wrong."

"Mum, seriously, I need to tell you in person, so that I'm with you when I break the news to you."

"Oh my goodness, babe, now you've got me all worried. Can't you tell me now?"

"No, mum. Look, I have to go now, but I'll be with you as soon as I can."

"But."

Marlene ended the call, went back to the conservatory and held her phone out to WPC Tracy. "Please leave it on the coffee table, Marlene. The forensic team will put it in an evidence bag and the phone will be returned to you once they no longer require it."

Marlene took the keys to her dad's house off her key chain and placed them on the coffee table and left the house. She got into her car and drove toward her mum's house. As she drove, she contemplated the best way to break the news to her mum and how much of the truth she should tell her.

EPILOGUE

In just over seventy-two hours, Jane and Dan had managed to get to the bottom of who'd killed Christopher and why they'd killed him. She knew that Dan had ensured that justice had been served and it was only a question of time before Dan found out if he was going to be caught for the crime he'd committed or be allowed to live a free life. Every day, Dan's future hung in the balance, and it swayed from one side to the other, and she knew he was walking on a high tight rope.

Sylvia called Jane personally to thank her for everything she'd done to help them uncover the truth about who'd been responsible for killing her son. She assured Jane that things had been dealt with in an appropriate manner, but she stressed that the less Jane knew, the better it would be for her. Jane agreed and simply told her that she was glad that she and Ethan were satisfied with her services.

Even though Jane's work on the case had come to an end, she couldn't stop herself from trying to work out why Ricky the Rat had come to her assistance. From what she'd read about him, she hadn't been able to connect him to either Marlene or Ben. In an attempt to draw closure on the case, she made the assumption that Ben or one of his team had sourced the heroin from Ricky and then injected him with enough of it to cause him to overdose, so there was no risk of him being able to testify that he'd sold it to them.

Sylvia arranged for a very intimate ceremony to be held for

Christopher, and it was only attended by her, Patricia, Ethan, and Dan. It was a much more meaningful and emotional affair because all four of them knew they could finally put Christopher to rest, knowing their memories of him would live on with them until the day they died.

While Dan was still a free man, Sylvia insisted that Ethan and Dan have dinner with her at her house. It gave Sylvia a proper opportunity to express her thanks to Ethan and Dan for everything they'd done to find Christopher's killer and ensure that justice had been served. She hoped she'd be able to draw closure on Christopher's death, mourn properly, and try to rebuild her life without Christopher being a part of it.

During the evening, they reminisced on their fondest memories of Christopher, and they all did their best to make the evening a celebration of Christopher's life, rather than a morbid affair with lots of sadness and tears. There were times when emotions did run high, and some tears did flow, but in the main, it was a very positive and cheerful evening.

Given Sylvia knew Dan wasn't responsible for her son's death, she let her guard down a bit

Ethan saw the beginnings of a new friendship blossoming between the two of them.

During the following few weeks, Ethan and Dan were invited to Sylvia's house for dinner each week, and as they opened up about their feelings and emotions, the three of them started to form a special bond, because they all had one thing in common—they all loved Christopher dearly, and they were all mourning his passing in their own personal ways.

When the rental contract on Ethan's house came to an end, Sylvia insisted that he moved in with her for a while until he felt capable of facing the future on his own. He confessed he didn't relish the thought of being on his own, so he accepted Sylvia's invitation to spend some time living with her—just until he'd got his mind straight and was strong enough to tackle life on his own.

Dan deliberately stayed out of Marlene's way, but he spoke to some of his friends involved in the cage fighting scene who knew Marlene, and they assured him she hadn't spoken to any of them about what had happened.

After a month, Dan received an unexpected call from Marlene, and she let him know she'd kept to her side of the bargain and expected him to keep to his side of the bargain. Once she'd explained how she'd staged it to look as if a junkie had broken into the house looking for money and valuables and they'd been the person who'd killed her dad, he gave her his word he wouldn't talk to the police about what really happened.

Marlene assured Dan the police didn't find any conclusive evidence to convict anybody and while they were still pursuing the case, she suspected they'd close it down within a matter of weeks because they knew they stood as much chance of finding her dad's killer as they'd have to find a needle in a haystack.

To give him even more reassurances she wouldn't be encouraging the police to pursue the case any further, Marlene told Dan that once she and her mother had sold her dad's house they were both going to buy a property in Malaga so they could start a fresh life there and make some radical changes to their lifestyles. She joked that she had no intention of ever fighting again since Jane managed to kick her arse so quickly in the cage and that it didn't fit in with the new lifestyle she had planned for her, her mother, and Desmond.

Dan thanked her for her call and wished her every success

and happiness with her new life in Malaga. As far as Dan was concerned, the further she was away from England and the police, the better for him. Once she'd gone, he was confident the police would drop the case given their resources were being cut all the time. They couldn't afford to keep pursuing a case that had very little hope of being solved, and they probably knew enough about Ben's chequered past and dirty dealings to know there could be hundreds of people who had good reason to kill him.

As he grew in confidence, he'd get to spend the rest of his life as a free man, Dan made more of an effort to spend time with Ethan and Sylvia, and with time, the three of them became quite the happy family unit.

Ethan suspected that maybe one day, Dan and Sylvia might take their friendship to the next level, and he hoped for both their sakes that they did. It gave him reassurances that they'd be there for each other in times of need and it'd help them both fill a huge void in their lives with the loss of Christopher.

Ethan couldn't envisage himself ever meeting another man who'd compare to Christopher. But as time passed, Sylvia and Dan made it clear that if he did meet somebody as wonderful as Christopher and who meant as much to Ethan as Christopher had, then they would do everything they could to accept them and make them feel part of their close little family that they'd created with time. Ethan couldn't imagine ever meeting someone who he'd loved as much as Christopher, but Sylvia and Dan's support made him feel comfortable that he had the freedom to fall in love again if the opportunity ever presented itself in the future.

You may also enjoy the following from eXtasy Books Inc:

Shedding His Wings
LJ Collins

Excerpt

The alarm clock rang loudly in Jay's ears. He rolled over and reached out to turn it off. It was times like this he questioned why he worked as a police officer. He wasn't fond of getting up at two in the morning, but he had to get showered, dressed in his police uniform, and get to the operation candy sweep offices. They'd been planning a series of drug raids, and the sixth of June was the day for the dawn raid on a house in New Cross, south-east London.

It was three-thirty when Jay arrived at the offices. He parked his car, locked it, and walked toward the entrance of the building. When he reached the door, he buzzed the intercom system, stood in front of the camera, and held his officer's identity card at the side of his head.

After a few seconds, the door buzzed. Jay pushed it open and walked into the reception area. He greeted the security guards and walked to the automated barrier entry system where he swiped his card, then walked through when the barrier opened.

Jay took the elevator to the eighth floor. When the doors opened, he got out and walked toward the candy sweep operation room. He turned the door handle, opened the door and walked into the room. All heads turned in his direction. There were five people sat around the conference table. Jay instantly recognised his long-term partner in crime, Ricky. One of the other faces was familiar, but he'd never seen the other people.

Detective Chief Inspector Hawkins was sat at the head of the table facing him. He looked at Jay and beckoned him to join them. "We're still waiting for a couple of the armed officers to arrive, Jay. Take a seat and talk among yourselves while we're waiting."

Jay nodded, walked toward the conference table and sat next to Ricky. He patted him on the shoulder and smiled. "How ya doing, buddy?"

"Yeah, I'm cool. Fired up and raring to go."

"So you think we're gonna score tonight?"

"I bloody hope so. The little shit has been dealing for way too long. I can feel it in my water tonight's gonna be our night. He needs to be put down, and fast. It makes me sick knowing he's selling drugs to young kids. What kind of scumbag pushes drugs at schools?"

Jay shook his head. "The lowest of the low, mate. But that's why we joined the drug squad. To make sure the streets of London are cleaned up and made a safer place. And so that unscrupulous evil monsters like Andy Pearson are put away for good."

"Yeah. Well, I'm taking tonight personal."

"What do you mean by that?"

Ricky blew out air and shook his head. "Don't tell Hawkins, but my daughter and her best friend went to a festival at the weekend."

"And?"

"And . . . some fucker sold her friend some gear that completely screwed her up. She's been in a coma for two days, and the doctors don't know what she'll be like when she comes out of it. I'm just so thankful my baby's got more sense and doesn't take drugs. By Christ, I've warned her enough times about the dangers of taking them. Some of the shit on the street these days is lethal and has killed young kids. I've seen things on the TV and social media. Kids are taking their lives into their own hands these days when they take drugs."

"Yeah. You don't need to tell me. I'm fully aware."

The door handle clicked. Jay turned, and two officers walked into the room.

DCI Hawkins cleared his throat. "Right, come on guys. Sit yourselves down, and then we can make a start."

The two officers sat down on the first available seats facing Jay and Ricky.

DCI Hawkins stood up. "Right, ladies and gents. I've had an update from the two plain-clothed officers who've been keeping Andy Pearson's property under surveillance since nine this evening. At the moment, it's not good news for us. His girlfriend is with him, along with two other men, and we don't know who they are. They could be friends, Andy's dealers, or his supplier. I suspect it's not the latter, because a supplier is highly unlikely to go to a dealer's house no matter how big they are. The surveillance officers have confirmed nobody's left the house and there are no lights on inside. That indicates they've gone to bed. It's only a two-bedroom house, so one of the guys could be sleeping on the sofa. Failing that, they all got high and the two guys are in the same bed shagging the arse off each other."

All the officers, apart from Jay, laughed. He looked down at the table. His cheeks burned. He didn't know if he was more embarrassed that Hawkins had just outed him to people he didn't know, or if he was angry. Jay looked up and glared at DCI Hawkins.

"Oh dear. I'm sorry, Jay. I was just trying to make light of a difficult situation. Please don't take any offence."

Jay raised his eyebrows and tilted his head. "No offence

taken, sir. Us gays get it from all walks of life, so I've developed a tough skin over the years." Jay looked at the other officers in turn and smiled sarcastically.

"Anyway. Going back to tonight. The other guys aren't our priority for tonight. We'll take them into custody and question them, but let's focus on Andy."

An officer raised his hand.

"Yes, Marshall."

"Do we know if they're armed, sir?"

"Hmm. We can't be sure, but they could be. If not with guns, they'll probably have knives, machetes, or swords." DCI Hawkins looked around the table at each officer. "All of you be on guard. I don't want any casualties on our side. Expect the unexpected, work as a team, and take good care of each other. Understood?"

The officers nodded. "Right. I think you all know what the plan is, but let's have a quick recap. Ricky, Jay and WPC Collman—you're taking the back entrance. Focus on the kitchen and lounge. The rest of you will be going through the front door. As soon as you're in, go to the bedrooms. That's where most of them, if not all of them, are likely to be."

The officers nodded.

"Right. Get in there as fast as you can. I don't want Andy or his friends getting rid of the evidence before you detain them. Okay. So I think we're all clear about what needs to be done, so go and do what you do best." The bellow of cheers echoed around the room. "The van is waiting downstairs for you in the car park. Go, be careful, and I wish you all the luck in the world."

The officers cheered, stood up and walked toward the door. Jay and Ricky introduced themselves to WPC Collman. As they made their way to the car park, they worked out their game plan.

ABOUT THE AUTHOR

Born and raised in London, Lee worked as a successful senior management consultant before moving to Tenerife to pursue a more fulfilling life and focus on his writing.

www.ingramcontent.com/pod-product-compliance
Lightning Source LLC
Chambersburg PA
CBHW070831120626
46556CB00002B/718